oasis

DON'T LOOK BACK

Alison James

sona
BOOKS

sona BOOKS

© Danann Publishing Limited 2024

First Published by Danann Media Publishing Limited 2024
WARNING: For private domestic use only, any unauthorised Copying, hiring,
lending or public performance of this book is illegal.

CAT NO: SON0605

Photography courtesy of

Getty images:

Dan Callister/Liaison
DAN CALLISTER Online USA Inc
Gareth Davies
Dave Hogan
Giuseppe Cacace
Tim Mosenfelder
Dave Benett
John Gunion/Redferns
Des Willie/Redferns
Patrick Ford/Redferns
Steve Catlin/Redferns
Roberta Parkin./Redferns
Paul Bergen/Redferns
Suzie Gibbons/Redferns
Donna Santisi/Redferns

Mick Hutson/Redferns
Michael Ochs Archives
Michael Putland
Larry Hulst/Michael Ochs Archive
Jeff Kravitz/FilmMagic
Michel Linssen/Redferns
Edd Westmacott/Avalon
Joe Dilworth/Avalon
Scott Heavey
Lucas Oleniuk/Toronto Star
Martyn Goodacre
Pete Still/Redferns
Ebet Roberts/Redferns
Engelke/ullstein bild
Peter J Walsh/PYMCA/Avalon

Brian Rasic
Independent News and Media
Howard Walker/Mirrorpix
Bill Rowntree/Mirrorpix
Sergione Infuso/Corbis
Paul Natkin
Luciano Viti
Roberto Panucci/Corbis
Javier Bragado/WireImage
Mariano Regidor/Redferns
Niels van Iperen
Koh Hasebe/Shinko Music
Shirlaine Forrest/WireImage
James Fry
Live From Abbey Road/Michael Gleason

Alamy:

PA Images
TCD/Prod.DB
TT News Agency

Jeff Gilbert
Rob Watkins
WENN Rights Ltd

CBW
dpa picture alliance

Other images, Wiki Commons

Book design Darren Grice at Ctrl-d
Proof reader Juliette O'Neill

Made in EU.
ISBN: 978-1-912918-64-5

contents

chapter 1
THE BROTHERS GALLAGHER

'We were just lads from a council estate'

Noel Gallagher

t was a random telephone call that started it all. Made on a Sunday evening in summer 1991. Inspiral Carpets' roadie, Noel Gallagher was on tour with the band in Munich and, as he did every Sunday, had called his mum, Peggy, at home in Burnage, Manchester. Chatting away about family matters, Noel asked his mum how his younger brother, Liam, was.

'Oh, he's out rehearsing,' came the reply.

'What for?' asked Noel. 'He's not joined the Shakespeare f**king group, has he?'

'Oh no,' Peggy said. 'He's in a band – he's the singer.'

'He's the singer?' Noel was aghast. 'He can't f**king sing!'

It wasn't until Noel returned home a few weeks later and went to see Liam's group play, that he realised his brother could sing. . . and more.

'I was shocked at him on stage – he didn't look out of place,' Noel later said. 'The band were good. I thought they had something.'

It was a wake-up call for Noel. He'd always been the Gallagher brother who was into music. Obsessed, in fact. His older brother. Paul, had dabbled before jacking it in but Liam, five years Noel's junior, had never expressed much interest.

MAIN IMAGE: Cranwell Drive, Burnage, Manchester, the street where the Gallagher brothers used to live

'All those years I'd spent sharing a room with him and I'd be sat playing a guitar and he'd just be sat staring at me, going, 'Lend us a fiver, lend us a fiver, lend us a fiver. . .' said Noel.

Noel and Liam were polar opposites. Noel, born in May 1967, was moody, self-contained and a day-dreamer while Liam, born five-and-a-half years later in September 1972, was a show-off and a scally who constantly demanded to be the centre of attention.

'I don't know why me and Liam would be so different – we both had the same childhood and I could never work it out,' said Noel.

The three sons of Irish Catholic immigrants Tommy and Peggy Gallagher had hardly enjoyed a happy childhood. Tommy was an alcoholic and a womaniser who was violent and abusive towards his three sons and their mother. Paul and Noel were so badly affected as small boys that both developed stammers, which were only cured after four years' speech therapy. Liam, however, got off more lightly.

'He only hit me once,' he recalled. 'But I watched it – and watching it can be as bad as copping it. Watching it is mad, it's mental. There were s**t times growing up.'

"He only hit me once"

Peggy acquired a legal notice of separation from her husband in 1976. Eight years later – much of them filled with abuse towards her and the boys – she finally left him, taking the three lads with her. Keeping it secret from Tommy, Peggy had been allocated another council house after a very long wait.

'The new house was in a terrible state with no paper on the walls and just bare floorboards but I wasn't bothered,' she said. *'I'd sooner live like that with just the floorboards because we had peace at last.'*

Peaceful it may have been but Peggy's sons – and in particular Noel and Liam - gave her endless trouble. The Gallagher brothers regularly played truant from school – with Noel being especially talented at bunking off and not getting caught, even when Peggy started working as a dinner lady at his secondary school, St Marks. Noel would go to school for registration before leaving for the morning. He'd return at lunchtime, making sure that Peggy saw him – preferably in the company of a teacher. After lunch, he'd bunk off again and return home at the normal time. He managed this routine for the best part of a term, spending the time at his friends' houses, listening to records and sniffing glue.

'Me mam was flabbergasted at the military precision of how I managed to blag a whole term of school when she thought I was in every single day,' said Noel. *'I think she admired me for that!'*

TOP LEFT: Family portrait of the Gallagher family in the mid 1970's from left to right Noel, Paul, Liam and Mum Peggy Gallagher.
TOP RIGHT: Tommy Gallagher, 1997

By now music was beginning to play a major part in the 13-year-old's life.

'It was a gradual thing to do with music – the Beatles had always been there and were a massive influence. For my generation, we went from seeing T Rex and Bowie on Top of the Pops to the '80s and beyond. It was a huge deal for me. I was into the Sex Pistols but was just too young for them. The first band I saw on TV – on the Old Grey Whistle Test – and had a connection with was The Jam. After that were The Smiths and New Order – and they were from Manchester. Mind-blowing! But the first band I saw and I thought, "I can do that" was the Stone Roses. It took off from there really.'

Not that he seriously considered a career in music at that stage.

'I wasn't ambitious - it didn't happen to people like me. There was no one like me on TV. How could it possibly happen? Where I come from in Burnage, I was the only person who was interested in anything other than Manchester City. When everyone else was experimenting with cars and drinking lager, I was going to town to see bands and stuff like that. They thought I was a weirdo. Manchester gave me a great musical education: New Order, the Smiths, Happy Mondays, Joy Division and the Stone Roses were all from there – great bands that gave me something to aspire to. Music was an escape for me – it took me away for three minutes from cold, boring Northern England.'

Noel had already taken up the guitar and although left-handed, played right-handed.

'Me mam was always grounding me because I was always bunking off school and getting caught smoking and f**king glue-sniffing and robbing - all the usual '70s, '80s gear - and I had absolutely nothing to do. Everyone was going out and I couldn't be bothered doing my f**king homework so I just sat there playing one string on this acoustic guitar that had been behind the back door – no one knows how it got there. I used to play one string and then it kind of just went from there. I learned to play Joy Division bass lines on one string. Then I went to two strings and then three, then four. . . The first song I learned to play was House of the Rising Sun by the Animals. Once I could play a couple of chords, the next thing was to write a song. It wasn't an instant thing and I never used to stand in front of the mirror with a tennis racket. I never thought I would become a rock star.'

FROM TOP LEFT CLOCKWISE: The Beatles; The Stone Roses; T Rex; David Bowie; The Sex Pistols

Leaving school at 15, Noel started working for his father in the construction industry. Not surprisingly, given their tempestuous relationship, it didn't work out. He then took a labouring job at another building firm sub-contracted to British Gas. While there, the bones in his right foot were broken when a heavy cap from a steel gas pipe landed on it.

'That was a pivotal moment in my life,' he says. *'When I came back from the sick, they gave me a cushy job in stores handing out bolts and wellies. Nobody would turn up for days on end. After about six weeks I started bringing my guitars in and I wrote four of the songs from the first album in that storeroom.'*

In May 1988, Gallagher met guitarist Graham Lambert of Manchester Indie band Inspiral Carpets at a Stone Roses show. They got talking when Noel saw Lambert recording a bootleg of the gig and Noel asked for a copy. They became friends with Noel regularly going to Inspiral's gigs. When he heard singer Steve Holt was leaving the band, Gallagher auditioned to be the new vocalist. He didn't get the gig

'Couldn't sing a f**king note,' he was later to say. *'I did Gimme Shelter, shouting me head off like Shaun Ryder, and they turned me down.'*

As consolation, he was offered a role as a roadie and immediately accepted. For the next two years, he travelled the world with the band.

'Noel's time with the band was like his Youth Training Scheme,' wrote older brother Paul. *'At 21 and 22, it gave him ample opportunity to expand his musical dexterity and get paid for looking after, setting up and playing about with guitar, bass, keyboards and drums. The fact that he could fiddle about with instruments during sound-checks and rehearsals and all those hours on end in various studios, meant that by the time Noel left, he'd more or less mastered every instrument. With his bowl haircut and loud, big-patterned shirts, Noel ended up looking like one of the Inspirals and ended up like a member of the band. He roadied for them, sorted out the T shirts and merchandising, worked in their management office and took care of the groups soundchecks. That's how Noel became close mates with Mark Coyle who was the Inspirals sound-man.'*

Mark and Noel bonded over their love of the Beatles, and the pair spent sound-checks dissecting the group's songs and rehearsing Noel's own material.

'The worst thing was knowing that I was miles better than the Inspirals – miles better. But I needed the money and I stuck it hard 'cos getting a band off the ground is difficult.'

"Couldn't sing a f**king note"

MAIN IMAGE: Steve Holt and Inspiral Carpets live

LEFT: Noel Gallagher working as a roadie for the Inspiral Carpets, Manchester, 1992

Liam, meanwhile, was getting into trouble. At secondary school, he was the worst of the bad boys - getting into fights, drinking, drugging, and robbing. Even at primary school he'd been a nightmare with his teacher telling Peggy that she needed to take a tranquiliser every evening after spending the day with him.

'I paid more visits to that (secondary) school over Liam than I can remember,' Peggy recalls. *'They expelled him at the age of 15 – I can't remember exactly what it was for. He was out of school for three months because the head teacher refused to have him back. I had to go back to the school and grovel again to the headmaster for them to take him back.'*

When he finally left school five months later, he got a job at a fencing company but left after three weeks. Various other transient labouring jobs followed but he ended up on the dole. He did, however, believe he would be famous.

'He used to say, "I'll be famous one day, Mam, and you'll be proud of me",' Peggy recalls. *' "'I wasn't put on this earth to dig holes. I was put on this earth for something special. I can feel it in my bones". I used to tell him to come down from the clouds, that he was living in cloud cuckoo land.'*

He wasn't at all interested in music as yet. According to his eldest brother, Paul, *'Our Liam never liked guitar music or guitar bands. He thought they were all twats.'*

'I wasn't interested in music and when I saw someone with a guitar I'd boot the bottle at him - I thought they were weird, God squad and all that,' said Liam. *'I just played football and came home late for my tea. I knocked on people's doors and ran off. Ran through people's garden and nicked things like clothes off the washing line if I thought they looked pretty cool. Mountain bikes, lawn mowers – anything. I'd sell 'em for weed.'*

Liam's musical 'lightbulb' moment came when he was 17 and 'discovered' the Stones Roses, admittedly two or three years later than everyone else in Manchester.

'I saw the Stone Roses – they looked like us, they didn't have leather keks on and stuff like that, d'you know what I mean? They wore clothes like we wore in the park. That was it for me. That was my epiphany. Ian Brown, John Squire, the lads. . . You don't have to wear leather keks and pointy shoes to be in a band. They were playing this magical music. Maybe it was the drugs, but I think it was the music as well.'

"I saw the Stone Roses, they looked like us"

MAIN IMAGE: Ian Brown performing with The Stone Roses, London, 1987

Liam wanted to be the next Ian Brown. His opportunity came when a local band called the Rain fired their lead singer. Liam knew the other members – guitarist Paul 'Bonehead' Arthurs, Tony McCarroll on drums and bassist Paul 'Guigsy' McGuigan – and sorted an audition. Rain wanted Liam to join their ranks but he refused unless they changed the name of the band. He suggested Oasis, from an Inspiral Carpets' poster than had been on his and Noel's bedroom wall, advertising their gig at Swindon Oasis. The first gig the newly-formed Oasis played was supporting a combo called Sweet Jesus at the Boardwalk on Little Peter Street in Manchester on August 18 1991. Noel was in the audience and, for the first time, realised that 'Our kid' had something. But Noel had something they wanted.

'The first thing they said when they came up to me was, "What do you think?" I said, "F**king great",' Noel was to recall. 'They said, "We were thinking, would you fancy being our manager?" I was like, "What? What the f**k are you talking about? No." And they were like, "Because you know loads of people, and all that". I said, "Not sure about that. I think you'd get a better manager than me". Then a couple of weeks later Liam said, "Come and f**king jam with us". So, I went and sat in with them and I was playing their tunes and it was great. And then I think the second time I went, Liam was going, "Play them that f**king song that you played us".'

The song was 'All Around the World'.
Noel was blown away.

'And then once everybody all joined in and you hear this thing that you've in inverted commas "written" being played back to you in this room and it's like, "Wow! F**king hell! That's amazing!" So, I went and joined them – and the rest is history.'

Not quite yet it wasn't. . .

MAIN IMAGE: Oasis Original Line Up, 1993

chapter 2
THE EARLY YEARS

'And then for two years it went nowhere'

Noel Gallagher

Oasis couldn't have come at a better time for Noel. Within months of joining his brother's band, he'd been 'let go' by the Inspiral Carpets. According to Paul Gallagher, this was because Noel had his own ambitions and the Inspirals felt his heart wasn't in the job any more. He had, however, been given a pay-off of £2000 which delighted Liam.

'Our Liam's reasons for wanting Noel in were – money, a lead guitarist, experience and probably lastly, songs,' said Paul.

But Liam also knew the band needed Noel's talent as a song writer.

'We knew we wouldn't get any better unless we had his songs – and his guitar playing and stuff, you know.'

As for Noel, he had long wanted to perform with his own band. He knew he could write songs, knew he could play guitar and, thanks to being part of the Inspiral's crew for some years, had some insight into how the music business functioned.

MAIN IMAGE: Liam and Noel Gallagher, 1993

'*Being with the Inspiral Carpets was a great chance to suss it all out for three or four years,*' he said. '*Being around managers, agents, record company people, journalists. . . I'd just sit there never saying a word to anyone.*'

With Oasis, however, Noel laid down the law. He insisted Oasis came first. They would give it their all. No one would miss rehearsals, and their drink and drug intake needed watching. Rumour had it that he'd insisted they would play only his songs. He was the only writer and his word was law – although he was later to dispute this.

'*So, I mean, there is the myth that I kicked open the f**kin' rehearsal door to the theme tune to "The Good, the Bad, and the Ugly", and said, "Everybody, stop what you're doing. I am here to make us all millionaires". You know, it wasn't that at all. I never said to anyone else, "You are not allowed to write songs, this is my thing".*'

Maybe not, but it clearly was 'his thing'. He had loads of songs and parts of songs that he'd written over the years, and lost no time in integrating them into the band's set.

They played one number - 'Take Me' which had been penned by Liam and Bonehead - at the Granada Television festival in October 1991, although they nearly didn't make it on stage as Liam had an altercation with actor Simon Gregson (Coronation Street's Steve McDonald) who'd almost – accidentally – run him over in the carpark. When Liam started yelling, Gregson flicked the vs with the result that Liam lost it and started shouting, '*Come out here you t**t and I'll f**king knock you out.*' The actor had the sense to drive off.

Oasis played their first proper gig as a five-piece on January 15 1992 at the Boardwalk. It was not, by all accounts, a particularly memorable debut although, according to Paul Gallagher, '*with their new lead guitarist they certainly looked and sounded more like a rock n roll band with a mission*'. There weren't many in the audience but Noel seemed sure of the band's destiny.

'*There was 40 people maximum,*' he was later to tell Q magazine, '*and we had a song called "Rock and Roll Star. . . People were going, "Yeah, course you are, mate – bottom of the bill at the Boardwalk on a f**kin' Tuesday night." Pretentious a**eholes is what they thought we were. Went down like a f**king knackered lift. We thought they were going to be in raptures. And it ended in a bowl of silence. But from the first gig on, I don't know what came over us. We knew we were the greatest band in*

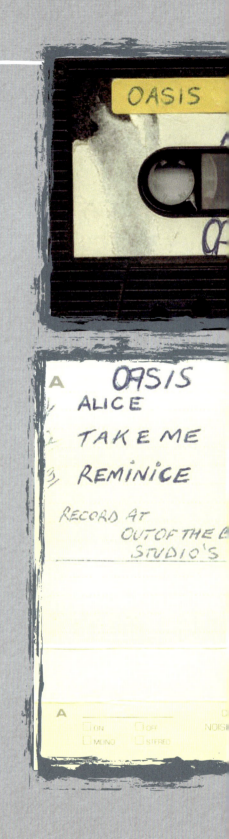

"... I'll f**king knock you out"

the world. We'd go, "F**king Happy Mondays, Stone Roses, they haven't got the tunes we've got. . .'

Gigs were slow in coming, so at Noel's bidding, the band recorded a demo which unfortunately failed to feature any of his compositions as he felt they had not rehearsed them to a high enough standard. According to Paul Gallagher, Noel later tried to distance himself from the tape which comprised of three Liam/Bonehead compositions - 'Alice', 'Reminisce' and 'Take Me'.

'He said in an interview before the band's two sell-out gigs at Maine Road (in 1996) that he didn't play on it,' wrote the eldest Gallagher brother, 'but I can tell you Noel played lead guitar on all the tracks.'

The demo was sent out but gleaned little interest. It was tough going but towards the end of the year – having played around eight gigs in 1992 – Oasis were occasionally headlining at the Boardwalk and had increased their audiences to around 100.

'At first, we did sound rough,' Noel was later to say. 'A lot of people did say we were like some mad punk band. I think we were writing so many songs so quickly, that we didn't realise we should be spending more time working on them, putting that bit there and this bit here on the chorus. Then one day we just got up and wrote our first pop song "Whatever", and I knew we'd have to wait before we could do it justice.'

By March 1993 and now rehearsing several times a week, the band were gigging more regularly – even venturing beyond Manchester to Liverpool on occasion where they went down a storm. As time passed they became more committed. One Saturday, Bonehead had been invited to a friend's wedding but he couldn't attend, he explained, because it was rehearsal day.

'The way it worked at rehearsals,' remembers Bonehead, 'was that Noel would always come in with something new and then we would jam on it. But you didn't miss rehearsals for anything. We totally believed in the band and the only way it was going to work was by grafting at it.'

'We never gave up,' recalls Liam. 'If nothing else we were dedicated. Yeah, I loved it. I loved it. That was when we were on our own for a bit, when everyone else was in "The Haçienda", popping pills and that, and all my mates would be knocking on the door, going, "What are you doing now?" "I'm going down the f**king rehearsal room". We weren't the best musicians but we had spirit, man, and that was lacking massively

ABOVE: Early Demo, recorded at Out Of The Blue Studios

anywhere else at that point. I always thought we were greater than the sum of our parts, you know what I mean? Bonehead? He was kind of the glue that held it all together. If anything, I'd say Bonehead was the spirit of Oasis. He's a top musician and can play anything but he's a mental c**t and I loved his mad side. So, me and him would get up to mad s**t together, you know what I mean? Guigsy? Guigs brought a calmness to it all. He never got flustered. He loved cricket and Doctor Who, and weed and Man City. I'd say fifth after that was being in Oasis – I'd say that came a lowly fifth. Guigsy – chilled out mother**ker, man. Lovely lad but just a complete and utter f**king stoner. Tony was the person I shared a room with in the early days, you know, and I really got on with Tony. Really nice person – very Irish in his ways, you know, came from a massive Irish family. Definitely the quiet one – the one who was most reserved.'

Finally, in May 1993, they got a break and found themselves a manager.

'I used to see this lad, Ian, down the Haçienda all the time in the late 1980s and we'd chat and have a laugh,' said Noel. 'When I bumped into him in town one day he asked, "What are you doing now?" I told him I'd got a band called Oasis. "Oh right," he said. 'You'll have to get us a tape and I'll play it to our kid". I just thought, Big deal.'

But Ian's 'our kid' was none other than Noel's childhood hero, Johnny Marr.

'I dragged Ian round to my flat and gave him a cassette,' Noel continues. 'Two hours later the phone rang. It was Johnny Marr himself. He'd heard our tape. Johnny helped us quite a lot, getting us a top professional manager. After he came to see us he actually phoned Marcus (Marcus Russell, whose Ignition management company looked after Johnny, Bernard Sumner from New Order and the Finn brothers from Crowded House).'

It was that same month that Oasis travelled to Glasgow to play at King Tut's Wah Wah Hut. They'd heard about the gig from an all-girl band called 'Sister Lovers' with whom they shared a rehearsal room. Unbeknown to Oasis, one of the girls in the band, Debbie Turner, was an ex girlfriend of Alan McGee's who ran Creation Records – 'the coolest record label in England' – and had 'Primal Scream' and 'The Jesus and Mary Chain' on his books.

AVOVE: Jonny Marr
TOP RIGHT: Sister Lovers
RIGHT: Marcus Russell

"It was Johnny Marr himself"

'We were like, "Well, how the f**k have you got a gig and not us?",' Liam remembers saying to Debbie. 'She said, "Why don't you come with us? Be on the bill, kind of thing". And we were like, "Yeah, Glasgow? F**k it, let's do it". For the pure love of it. "If we all put in 25 each, we can hire a splitter van, do the gig, sleep in the back. Yay!" So, we hired a van out, smoking weed, all that nonsense, drinking. You know one of them days where you just go, "It's f**king going to be the day today".' Maybe it was the drugs or something. We get there really early and we say, "We're Oasis from Manchester – we've come to play tonight." And the guy says, "There's a no band down here". I said, "Yeah, yeah, it's all right, we're with Debbie". And he's like. "No, no, no, no, no f**king way".

Or in the words of drummer Tony O'Carroll. . .

'"Neva heed of ye, now feck off!" The wrong thing to say to a vanload of hooligans come musicians who've spent their limited money getting there and taken a day off to boot. . . BigUn (a mate) starts the questioning. "Who owns the club, d**khead? Get him out here now. Tell him his club is getting f**king razed. Don't be a smart c**t. Sort it out". A verbal barrage, the arrows of mob rule. The door staff were shocked by the onslaught. So, as if doing us a favour, they let us in. There was a small crowd present as we made our way to the stage.'

In the 'small crowd' was Alan McGee, head of Creation Records – or 'The Prince of Pop' as he'd coined himself. He'd seen Oasis milling around and had mistaken Liam, whom he later described as 'looking like an 18-year-old Paul Weller' for the band's drug dealer.

'So, the promoter lets them play,' said McGee. 'Now, I wouldn't have got to see them normally, because when a band of mine's playing I usually get in five minutes before they come on stage. However, because I'd gone with my sister Susan, who doesn't happen to own a watch, I got there two hours early. I witnessed all the shenanigans, so I wanted to see what they were like. The first song was really good but I'd had, by this point, about four or five double Jack Daniels and coke, so I was, like, a bit wavery. But then the second was incredible. By the time they did this fantastic version of "I Am the Walrus", I'd decided I've got to sign this group, now. I said: 'Do you have a record deal? Do you want one? I wanna do it.'

Noel remembered it rather differently.

'We came on and, midway through our second song, he jumped on stage, came straight up to us and went, "Have youse got a record deal, man?" And we went "No!"'

Liam recalls. . .

'We thought he was taking the piss, 'cos he was all Armani'd up – a bit of a smoothie, like. And he said to me, right, to this day, he doesn't even know what the f**k he signed the band for. Something got him in there, he got butterflies in his stomach.'

What 'got' McGee was the belief that he'd just seen the greatest rock and roll band in the world – and he woke up record label staff in the middle of the night to tell them so. He bought the band train tickets to go down to London and see him a few days later.

'Bonehead, Liam and I went down to see Alan at Creation in London,' Noel remembers. *'We were expecting it to be this big flash office. We got in a cab at Euston station and ended up in Hackney. Even the dogs wore shoes, there was that much broken glass about. It was a totally dead and derelict-looking part of town. We went up to this big green door hanging off its hinges and knocked on it. We rang the intercom bell and there were sparks flying out of it. It was like the three stooges with Liam, Bonehead and me instead of Larry, Curly and Moe. When we went into Creation, it was like a rubbish tip with empty bottles everywhere and people asleep. We went down to Alan McGee's office which was called the bunker, with a big door and a sign that read, "Alan McGee, President of Pop". We just went in and he sent his assistant across the road to the pub for some Jack Daniels and said, "D'ye like Rod Stewart?" I said, "Yeah" and he said, "Right, you've got the deal". We just felt totally comfortable because they were all music fans.'*

Oasis didn't sign with Creation for another few months – Noel wanting to ensure that Marcus Russell was in place as their manager, and to also be certain about everything himself. As his brother, Paul, noted, *'Noel was very shrewd'.* Also, a late starter. He hadn't joined a band until he was 24 and now his first recording contract had come at 27.

'They all die at 27,' he said referring to the infamous '27 Club' whose members, at that time, included Jimi Hendrix, Jim Morrison and Brian – all of whom had passed away at 27. *'I was only just kind of limbering up then.'*

RIGHT: Oasis, 1993

"Right, you've got the deal"

"Creation have not gone mad"

In July 1993, the band played their last gig at the Boardwalk in Manchester. It had got out that Oasis had signed to Creation and the place was rammed. Afterwards, they had their first ever review in the national music press, published in the now defunct NME.

'Shout to the rooftops and dance in the streets – Creation have not gone mad! Lately they've been worrying us sick with the lack of pop product and bevy of rash signings, and the chances were that the latest "find" Oasis were going to be another nail in the "Where are Primal Scream?" band coffin. But no. Because Manchester's Oasis are genuinely a fine guitar-propelled pop band, with little of the crass baggage such a description suggests. They're not perfect, they might find it hard instinctively to impress, but they still stomp out the kind of terrifyingly memorable tunes that most bands forgot how to make as they blundered around on the periphery of true talent. Sound-wise they're slightly reminiscent of a drugged-up (ahem) version of the Stone Roses. It's almost as though everyone's favourite stroppily invisible Mancs have grown up and decided to take it slow this time, in the process swapping loon pants and T-shirts for sensible trousers and M&S pullovers. Mercifully, what they haven't mislaid is the basic brilliant melodic framework, as demonstrated by opener, 'Stray Dogs', with a rhythm involving more than three chords and a lyric concerned with driving your mates mad with jealousy because you're getting some bloke's lasagne (hopefully not a metaphor) and they're not. It's impossible not to be drawn in to take a closer listen. Bizarre shouts of "Showaddywaddy" from the floor are utterly unfounded. Good. With any luck, so are everyone's fears about the label that brought you the BMX Bandits. Even better, Oasis really are the shoots of vitality in a barren pop world.'

They were on their way. .

RIGHT: Oasis at Nomad Studios in Manchester, United Kingdom, 29th November 1993

MAIN IMAGE: L-R Paul McGuigan, Noel Gallagher, Tony McCarroll, Paul Arthurs (aka Bonehead), Liam Gallagher, November 1993

chapter 3

DEFINITELY MAYBE

*'Oasis was like a Ferrari - great to look at, great to drive. And it would f**kin' spin out of control every now and then'*

Liam Gallagher

Having landed the Creation deal, it was foot-on-the-gas all the way for Oasis – and in particular, the Gallagher bros.

'Once the Creation deal was in the bag, my brothers went into overdrive,' wrote elder brother Paul. *'They had a promo twelve-inch of Columbia, a favourite at their gigs, due out as a sampler in January 1994, with their first single proper due in the early spring. They wanted to be the biggest and the best in the world. Even though they fought and bitched about each other, they believed in each other's talents. I think Noel looked at Liam and to a certain extent wished he could be him and have that outward confidence and cockiness and, of course, be that age again. Liam really admired our Noel's ability on the guitar and wished he could write songs like him.'*

As far as was Noel was concerned, one of the most exciting elements about signing with Creation was Alan McGee's enthusiasm for his song writing.

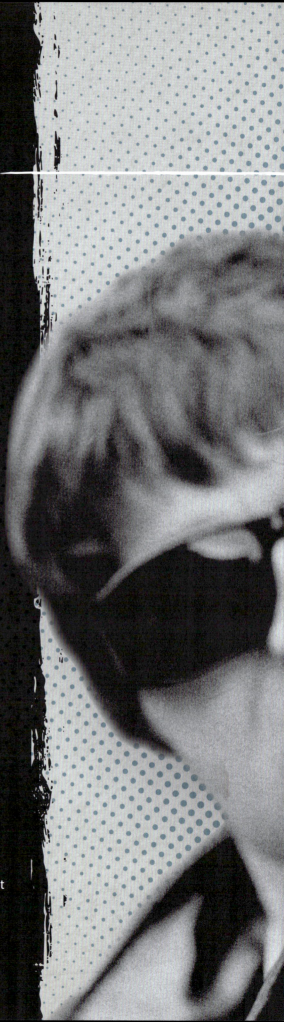

MAIN IMAGE: A portrait of Liam and Noel Gallagher, Netherlands, 1994

'I get a buzz from giving new songs to Alan because he actually thinks we're the greatest rock and roll band in the world,' he said. 'He phones me at four or five in the morning. I'll get out of bed and it's McGee on the other end enthusing, "I'm feeling supersonic, give me a gin and tonic… We're going to annihilate the world, man". That, in a nutshell, is why we're with Creation Records. Because the president is up at five in the morning reciting lyrics down the phone.'

The band were on the road for much of this period, supporting the likes of Saint Etienne and Primal Scream. While their following grew and they became tighter as a band, the brothers often clashed with obscenity-heavy slanging matches the norm – violence, too, on occasion. At a gig at Warwick University in December '93, Liam failed to turn up until the last minute. Noel was furious and lobbed a polystyrene chair at his brother's head. Fortunately, he missed. For the media, it was manna from heaven. Even before the release of Columbia, the record company were marketing the image of hell raising rock and roll siblings at each other's throats. After Warwick, came the band's first gig overseas – which made the headlines because it never actually happened.

'They were due to play in Amsterdam at the Sleep-In Arena with The Verve,' Paul Gallagher wrote. 'They were excited about it. It was Liam's first-ever trip outside the country and he was "mad for it", to use his own vernacular. The story is well documented. The boats going to the Hook of Holland have a disco on board and a bar going all night. The band were

"...We're going to annihilate the world, man"

MAIN IMAGE: L-R Paul Arthurs (aka Bonehead), Liam Gallagher, Noel Gallagher, Tony McCarroll, Paul McGuigan, 1993

TOP LEFT: Alan McGee

"It just wasn't happening..."

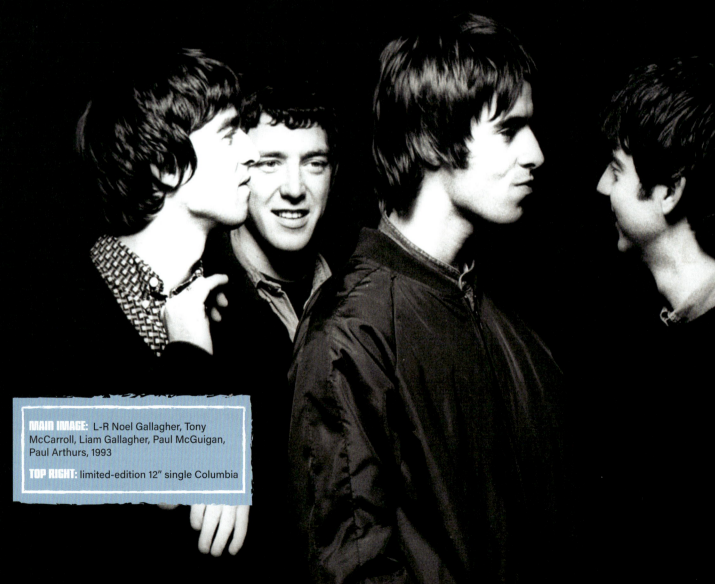

drinking during the eight-hour ferry trip, and Guigsy and Bonehead were singled out and accused of passing a fake £50 note over the bar. Despite protests, they were approached by security people and a fight broke out. The sound of any fight or argument immediately attracts our Liam who tried to calm things down by taking a swing at one of the boat's crew. They all ended up involved in a drunken brawl and were arrested. They were deported the next day – all of them, that is, except Noel who was sleeping in his cabin totally unaware of what was going on. He got off at the Hook of Holland and was left waiting for them at the port, not realising they'd been shipped back to England. He was more than just annoyed. They'd started living up to the reputation the press had given them but it meant the gig was cancelled. Noel might find it amusing now, but at the time I think all he could see was the group throwing it all away before they'd even had their first record out. I know he blamed Liam and must have been thinking it was Warwick University all over again, only much worse. He felt so let down he fined each band member £500, thinking that the only way to stop that behaviour was to hit them

MAIN IMAGE: L-R Noel Gallagher, Tony McCarroll, Liam Gallagher, Paul McGuigan, Paul Arthurs, 1993

TOP RIGHT: limited-edition 12" single Columbia

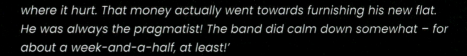

oasis

A. columbia (demo)

WRITTEN BY NOEL GALLAGHER

where it hurt. That money actually went towards furnishing his new flat. He was always the pragmatist! The band did calm down somewhat – for about a week-and-a-half, at least!'

The escapade made the Manchester Evening News and even News at Ten. It was unintentional yet inspired PR. Before Oasis had even released a record, they'd appeared on the national news. In late 1993 the limited-edition 12" single Columbia was released as a primer for journalists and radio programmers. Unexpectedly, BBC Radio One picked up the single and played it 19 times in the fortnight after its release. The band booked the £800-a-day Monnow Valley Studio, near Monmouth, to record their debut album. Their producer was Dave Batchelor, whom Noel Gallagher knew from Inspiral Carpet days. The sessions, however, were disappointing.

'It just wasn't happening,' Bonehead recalled. *'He was the wrong person for the job ... We'd play in this great big room, buzzing to be in this studio, playing like we always played. He'd say, "Come in and have a listen". And we'd be like, "That doesn't sound like it sounded in that room. What's that?" It was thin. Weak. Too clean. Noel was frantically on the phone to the management, going, 'This ain't working.' For it not to be happening was a bit frightening.'*

Batchelor was 'let go' and Noel tried to make use of the music already recorded by taking the tapes to a number of London studios. Tim Abbot of Creation Records said while visiting the band in Chiswick, west London. . .

'McGee, Noel, me and various people had a great sesh, and we listened to it over and over again. And all I could think was, "It ain't got the attack". There was no immediacy.'

It was decided the band should re-record the album.

'I'll always respect McGee for doing that,' Noel was later to say. *'He just said "F**king go and do it again because you've got to get it right".'*

In early 1994, the band set about re-recording the album at Sawmills Studio in Cornwall. This time the sessions were produced by Noel Gallagher and his friend Mark Coyle. They were pleased with the result but the record company wasn't. However, there was no chance of a third attempt at the album and the recordings already made had to be used. In desperation, Creation's Marcus Russell contacted engineer-turned-producer Owen Morris.

MAIN IMAGE: L-R Noel Gallagher, Paul Arthurs (aka Bonehead), Paul McGuigan, Tony McCarroll, Liam Gallagher, 1993

"'You can be a f*king knob like Joe Strummer...'"

'I just thought, 'They've messed up here,'' Morris recalled after hearing the Sawmills recordings. *'I guessed at that stage Noel was completely f**ked off. Marcus was like, "You can do what you like – literally, whatever you want".'*

Among the producer's first tasks was to strip away the layers of guitar overdubs Gallagher had added. Morris worked on mastering the album at Johnny Marr's studio in Manchester, and recalled that Marr was appalled by how *'in your face'* the whole thing was. The final mix took place in late May of '94.

As music journalist John Harris was to note, *'The miracle was that music that had passed through so many hands sounded so dynamic: the guitar-heavy stew that Morris had inherited had been remoulded into something positively pile-driving.'*

The band's first commercial single Supersonic had been released on 11 April 1994 and debuted the following week at number 31 on the British singles chart. This was followed by Shakermaker in June 1994, which debuted at number 11 and earned the group an appearance on Top of the Pops – which as kids, the band had been glued to every Thursday night.

'Top of the Pops? You've got to do it, you know what I mean?' said Noel shortly afterwards. *'You can be a f**king knob like Joe Strummer and say you're never going to do Top of the Pops. You've got to get on and do it and try and be as f**king big as you can. It's all about ambition, innit?'*

The same month, saw Oasis playing Glastonbury.

'It wasn't their best gig by any means,' wrote NME some years later,' *but it does show a band on the brink of greatness. Oasis went on to headline Glastonbury twice but neither performance could capture the laid-back swagger of their 1994 debut when Liam strutted onto the stage in a dreadful sweater and sang with a voice that was yet to feel the impact of too much booze and fags. They were still a year away from becoming the country's biggest rock band, but with a killer eight-song set - Shakermaker, Fade Away, Digsy's Dinner, Live Forever, Bring It on Down, Cigarettes & Alcohol, Supersonic, 'I Am the Walrus - there should have been no doubt as to where they were heading.'*

"...Yeah, that good"

Definitely Maybe was released on August 29 1994. The album sold 86,000 in its first week. On September 4, the album debuted at number one on the British charts. It outsold the second-highest album – The Three Tenors in Concert 1994 - by 50%. The first-week sales earned Definitely Maybe the record of being the fastest-selling debut album in British history. It received widespread critical acclaim along with commercial success, with many critics and listeners welcoming the album's fearless optimism while also praising Noel Gallagher's song writing and melodic skills along with younger brother Liam's vocals.

The NME called Noel Gallagher *'a pop craftsman in the classic tradition and a master of his trade'* and believed that *'the only equivocal thing about Definitely Maybe is its title. Everything else screams certainty. The fact is that too much heartfelt emotion, ingenious belief and patent song writing savvy rushes through the debut Oasis album for it to be the work of a bunch of wind-up merchants... It's like opening your bedroom curtains one morning and discovering that some f**ker's built the Taj Mahal in your back garden and then filled it with your favourite flavour of Angel Delight. Yeah, that good.'*

MAIN IMAGE: Noel and Liam Gallagher, at a photoshoot in a hotel in Tokyo, September 1994

ABOVE: Definitely Maybe album sleeve

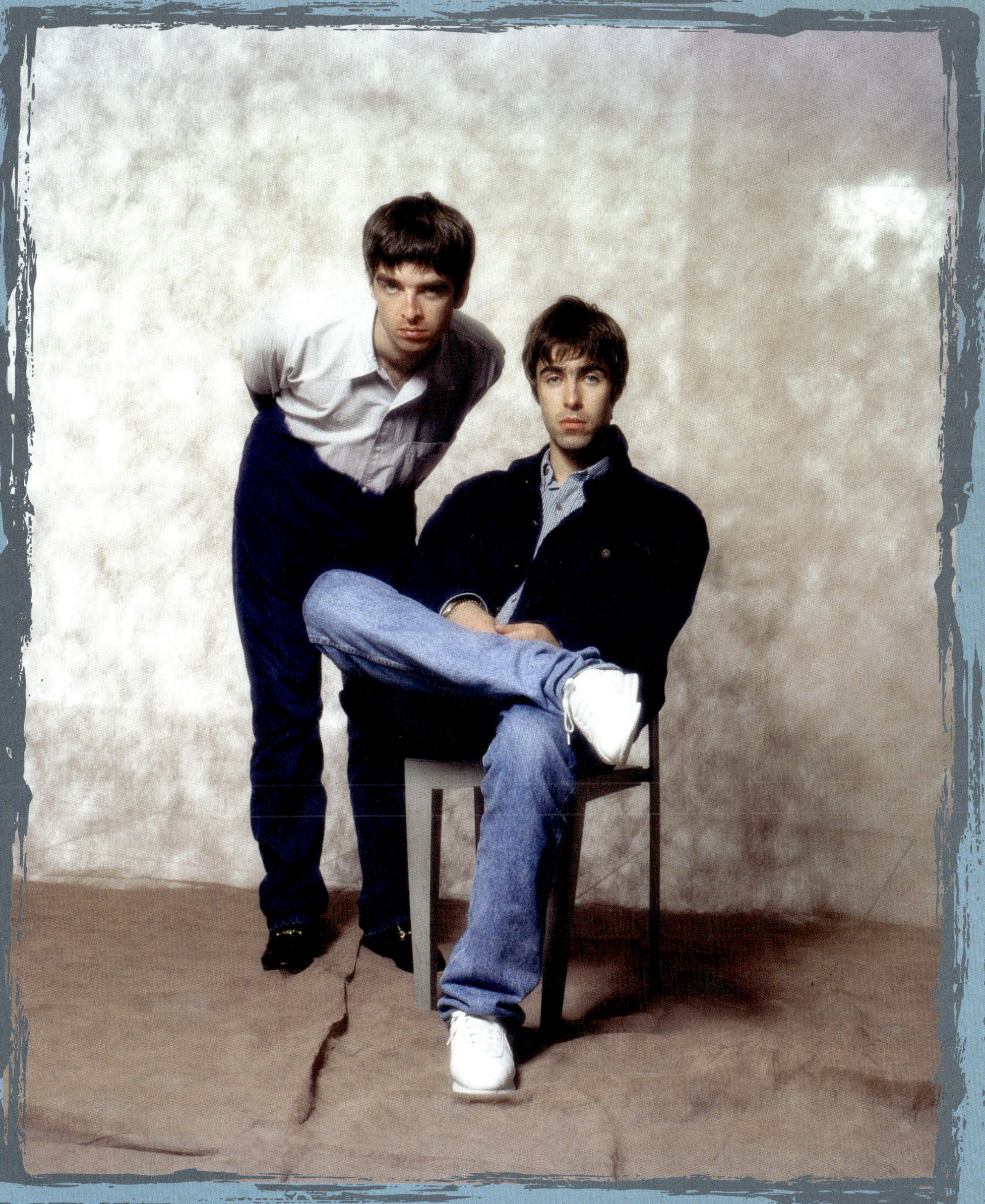

Melody Maker proclaimed the album a *'bloody essential'* purchase, adding that, *'Definitely Maybe is what the world's been waiting for, a record full of songs to live to, made by a gang of reckless northern reprobates who you can easily dream of joining'*. While Q magazine described the album as *'an outrageously exciting rock/pop album... A rutting mess of glam, punk and psychedelia - not since the Stone Roses debut have a young Lancastrian group carried themselves with such vigour and insouciance.'*

Such was Noel Gallagher's 'young Lancastrian's vigour', he shrugged off the fact that Coca Cola sued the band on the grounds that Shakermaker sounded like their 1971 advertisement tune I'd Like to Teach the World to Sing. His response? *'We just drink Pepsi now.'*

The album cover was something of a creative masterpiece in itself. An image of Noel's musical hero Burt Bacharach features in the bottom left of the artwork while the Clint Eastwood western The Good, the Bad and the Ugly – one of Noel's favourite films – plays on TV. A small photo of Manchester United legend George Best is on the window sill, Bonehead's defiant reminder that not every member of Oasis was a Manchester City fan. But, inevitably, if Bonehead was having a picture of a Manchester United player, the Gallagher brothers were going to have a bigger picture of Manchester City legend, Rodney Marsh.
'They were getting too big, too fast,' wrote Paul Gallagher. *'Oasis's success was phenomenal.'*

It was nothing less than Noel had expected.

'In 20 years' time our album Definitely Maybe will still be in the shops and that's what it's about,' he said prophetically in an interview he gave in 1994.' In 20 years' time people will buy the album and listen to it for what it is. They won't listen to it because we were rock'n'roll or something like that. That's what matters. Writing songs, that's what gets me going. Not the drugs or the sex or the rock'n'roll behaviour, it's the music.'*

The band continued touring, as they'd been doing for much of the year, playing at bigger and bigger venues. But it was during the US leg of the tour that Oasis came close to splitting. They were playing the legendary Whisky a Go Go club on Los Angeles' Sunset Boulevard. The night before the gig, the band took the drug Crystal Meth for the first time – although Noel was more restrained in his consumption than the rest of the band.

MAIN IMAGE: Liam in The Netherlands, 1994

"They were getting too big, too fast"

'We were still wired the next day,' drummer Tony McCarroll was later to recount. 'We had a gig that night, for f**k's sake. I turned up for the gig feeling terrible. The rest of the band were a mess, too. We plugged in and began the show. We had to start Rock n Roll Star twice because no one knew what the f**k was going on. Liam was barely audible, Noel's backing vocals were out of time and he forgot to start the intro. He and Bonehead were playing the wrong chords on the bridge and then Liam sang lyrics from a completely different song. Finally Guigsy's amp blew. Top f**king class! It seemed that everybody had different set lists so there was up to three different songs going on at the same time. Everyone was still meth-ed out of their heads. To make matters worse, Ringo Starr was watching from the crowd. Noel was looking round at everyone, obviously unhappy. Bonehead's reaction to the breakdown was to start taking photographs using a disposable someone had thrown on stage. He roared out laughing, with his thumbs up to the crowd. The gig went from bad to worse. Liam had a parcel of powder that he had put down behind my bass drum. In between songs, he was literally taking handfuls and troughing down, hidden behind my kit. Liam then turned back to face the crowd and screamed and contorted his face like he was in a wind tunnel.'

Liam threw his tambourine at Noel's head. It missed. But Noel was incandescent with rage. As soon as the shambles of the gig was over he walked off stage. After a massive row with Liam in the dressing room, Noel marched out and demanded the tour manager hand over the float – some $800 - and briefly returned to his hotel before leaving for San Francisco. He would not be heard nor seen of again for the best part of a week but was eventually persuaded to re-join the band. However, the dynamic had changed forever.

'I was in a fury – a little bit of me had left the stage that night,' Noel was later to say. 'After that it was more "me and them" as opposed to "us".'

The divide was clear to everyone.

'It started as soon as he walked back into the hotel and everything was different after that,' remembers Bonehead.'And we all had to be different because if we weren't with him, we'd be going home.'

A new era had begun. . .

MAIN IMAGE: Portrait of Noel Gallagher, 1995

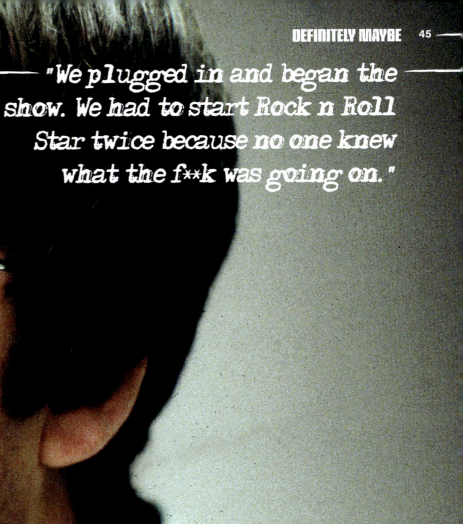

"We plugged in and began the show. We had to start Rock n Roll Star twice because no one knew what the f**k was going on."

chapter 4
MORNING GLORY

'The first album is about dreaming of being a pop star in a band. The second album is about actually being a pop star in a band'

Noel Gallagher

On December 18 1994, almost three months after the crystal meth incident – months in which the band had continued their US tour without any further serious disruptions or incidents - Oasis released their fifth single, Whatever, just in time for Christmas. It featured an orchestral arrangement of strings and reached number three in the UK charts.

'Two years ago, I told Melody Maker that Whatever would be a top five record round Christmas 1994,' said Noel in 1995. *'I knew it was going to happen. People slag off that belief, start calling it arrogant. What's wrong with arrogance? I know how good we are.'*

His confidence remained Teflon-coated even when he was once again sued for plagiarism, this time by British musician Neil Innes who claimed the song was exactly the same, in parts, to his Rutles' song, How Sweet to be An Idiot. Innes and Oasis settled out of court with Innes receiving a song-writing credit.

Talking retrospectively a year later Noel said of Whatever, '*I think this kind of wraps up the first part of Oasis, which is quite innocent and pure. It started to get very serious after that, we were kind of – a big rock band although we didn't feel it at the time.*'

In early '95, the band returned to the US to continue the tour, making a brief trip back to Britain in February for the Brit Awards. They'd been nominated in the Best Newcomer category – and they won, with the Kinks' Ray Davies presenting the band with the award. Noel thanked Ray for inspiring him, George Martin, who was in the audience, for producing '*the best band in the world*', ie, The Beatles, and, '*their parents*'. The other three didn't get to say anything, although Liam did later quip, '*We should have got more awards really. There isn't another band in the country that can touch us. And they know it.*'

BELOW: Portrait of Liam & Noel Gallagher, 1995
RIGHT: Oasis at The Academy in New York City on March 8, 1995

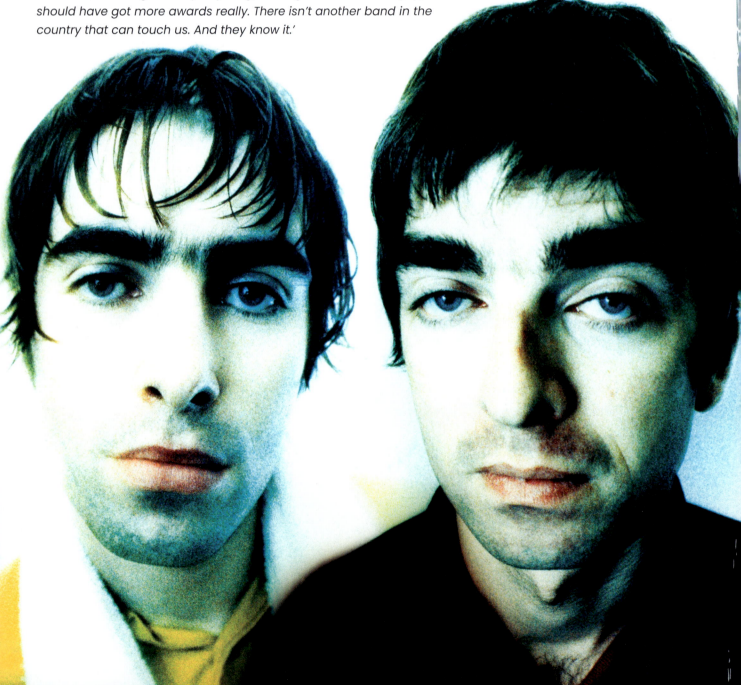

"I think this kind of wraps up the first part of Oasis..."

On April 22, Oasis returned from overseas, where they had continued to tour, to play their first Arena gig in Sheffield. Playing to 12,000 people, Oasis not only debuted Morning Glory on stage that night, but reportedly Noel had only started writing the song the night before. The story goes that he finished it off in the dressing room before taking to the stage. After the gig he remarked to a friend, *'Do you realise that a year ago we were just about to put our first single out and today we played to 12,000?'*

Three days later, the single Some Might Say was released. It went straight to number one, although it only stayed there for a week. But it was enough – for now.

'As soon as I'd written Some Might Say I was absolutely certain it would be a Number One and I was right,' Noel was to say in retrospect. *'I never had even the slightest doubt. It's the archetypal Oasis song. It defines*

"We needed a better drummer
so we got one"

what Oasis is. It proves we've done everything we said we would, and it's as much a success for our fans as it is for us. There are 10 bands in the top 10, five in the top five but there's only one at Number One!'

The Gallaghers, Guigsy and Bonehead were on a high but it was all over for drummer Tony McCarroll. He was ousted within a week of the single's release. It came as no surprise - tensions had been growing between McCarroll and the rest of the band for months, with Noel in particular questioning his ability as a drummer.

'It had been building up for ages. Tony had to go,' said Noel. 'When we got rid of Tony we didn't have a replacement and everyone was going, "You idiot, what are you going to do about the album?" because it was just before we were meant to start recording. And I was the only one who'd heard the songs because we don't do demos or any of that s**t, and I knew, well, I like Tony as a geezer but he wouldn't have been able to drum the new songs. People can say, "Oh you didn't give him a chance", and I didn't.'

Liam added, 'He wasn't a good drummer, that's the point. We needed a better drummer so we got one.'

This 'better drummer' was Londoner Alan White, brother of Paul Weller's drummer Steve White. An Oasis fan, he'd once walked out of one of their gigs because he didn't think much of the percussion. He was introduced to Noel by Weller on one Sunday, appeared on Top of The Pops by the Wednesday and had started recording the second album with the band by the weekend.

'We went out for a beer, came back and had a jam and that was it,' he recalls. 'I thought they'd be a bunch of nutses but they weren't, really.'

According to Noel, Whitey was, 'the new Keith Moon. Alan's great. We sit and watch him at sound-checks. I mean, nobody ever watches the drummer at sound-checks, especially not in our band.'

Oasis began recording material for their second album in Rockfield Studios near Monmouth with Owen Morris and Noel Gallagher producing. The band recorded the album quickly – initially anyway - averaging one song every 24 hours. However, tensions arose between Noel and Liam when Noel wanted to sing lead vocals on either compositions Wonderwall or Don't Look Back in Anger. Liam wasn't

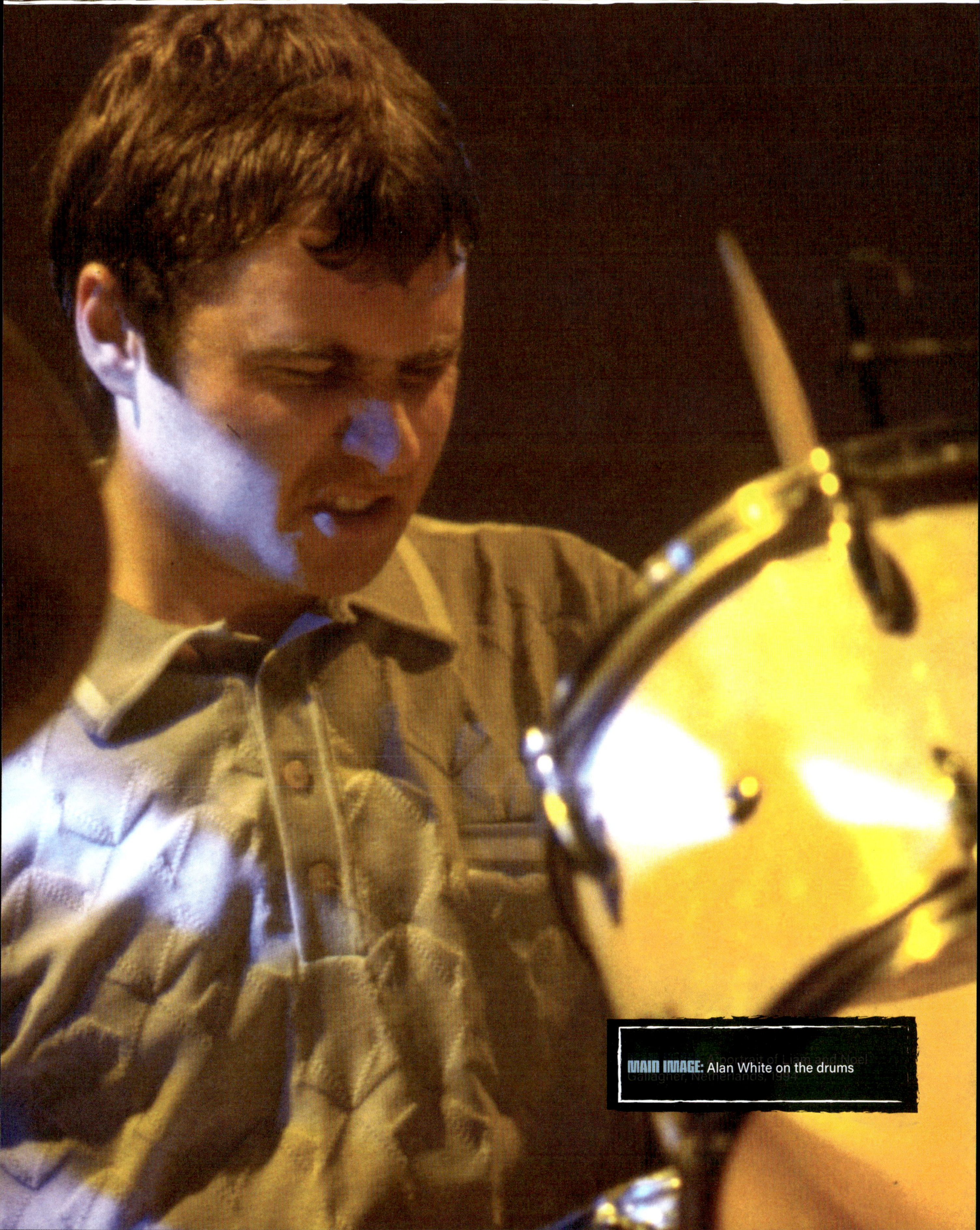

MAIN IMAGE: Alan White on the drums

"... *when Liam loses it, it's scary*"

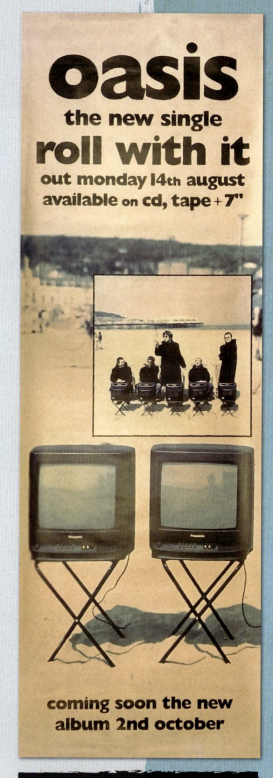

happy, feeling usurped as a vocalist and surplus to requirements. Matters improved a tad when Noel gave a thumbs-up to Liam's rendition of Wonderwall but he wasn't best pleased with Liam's strained attempts to sing the high notes on Champagne Supernova. When Noel then recorded his vocals for Don't Look Back in Anger, Liam huffed off to a local pub and came back with a crowd of very drunk people while recording was still underway. Noel was furious and ordered them all out but Liam was having none of it.

According to Owen, '*He lost it - and when Liam loses it, it's scary*'.

The brothers began fighting viciously with Liam trying to take charge of a couple of air rifles, fortunately Guigsy and Bonehead stopped him. He tried to smash up Noel's guitars with the result that Noel went after him

ABOVE: Roll With It promo poster
TOP LEFT: NME front cover, August 1995
RIGHT: Liam Gallagher out in London, 1995

with a cricket bat. When the fighting was over, leaving a wrecked studio, Noel took off and announced he was leaving – for the second time in 18 months. However, once both brothers had some breathing space, they reconciled and the band spent another two weeks working on the album, followed by post-production work in London.

Despite Liam and Noel's fight, Owen Morris was later to reflect, *'The sessions were the best, easiest, least fraught, most happily creative time I've ever had in a recording studio. I believe people can feel and hear when music is dishonest and motivated by the wrong reasons. Morning Glory for all its imperfection and flaws, is dripping with love and happiness.'*

The single chosen to precede the album's release was Roll with It, due out on August 1995, six weeks before the album was due to hit the shops. The managers of Blur, main Britpop rivals to Oasis, became worried that this would hinder the chances of the group's forthcoming Country House single reaching number one the following week. As a reaction, Blur's record company pushed the release of Country House back a week and thus started what became known as 'The Battle of Britpop'.

The event triggered an unprecedented amount of exposure for both bands in national newspapers and on television news bulletins, supposedly symbolising the battle between the middle class of the south, Blur, and the working class of the north, Oasis. In the midst of the battle a Guardian newspaper headline proclaimed, *'Working Class Heroes Lead Art School Trendies'*. In the event Country House outsold Roll with It by 54,000, and topped the singles chart for a fortnight. Overall singles sales that week were up by 41%. During a promotional interview in September, the month before the album was released, Noel spoke about the rivalry with Damon Albarn and Alex James from Blur but the interview ended disasterously for him

'I hope the pair of them catch AIDS and die because I f**king hate them two,' he said.

He later recanted, saying that AIDS was no laughing matter, but the quote caused a storm of controversy, with Noel having to write a letter of apology. He later confessed that *'my whole world came crashing down in on me then'*.

What's the Story Morning Glory was released on October 2 1995. The album sold very quickly with some record stores shifting copies at a rate of two per minute. At the end of the first week of sales, the album had sold a record-breaking 347,000 copies, making it - at the time - the second-fastest-selling album in British history, behind Michael Jackson's Bad. After initially entering the UK charts at number one, it hovered around the top three for the rest of the year before initiating a six-week stay at the top in mid-January, followed by a further three weeks at number one in March. In total, the album didn't leave the top three for an astonishing seven months. But if the fans loved it, critics were not sold on it. What's the Story Morning Glory was released to lukewarm reviews from the mainstream music press. Many contemporary reviewers expressed disappointment at the album's perceived inferiority to Definitely Maybe, taking aim at the *'banal lyrics'* and the unoriginal nature of the compositions.

A month before the album's release, the band had embarked on a lengthy world tour. But there were problems – not least that Guigsy was in a state of collapse, suffering a bout of exhaustion that left him unable to leave his bed. He was replaced by Scott McLeod, formerly of Manchester band The Ya Ya's. But McLeod couldn't hack it, and departed abruptly while on tour in the US. He later contacted Noel Gallagher claiming he felt he had made the wrong decision. Gallagher curtly replied '*I think you have too. Good luck signing on'.* To complete the tour, Guigsy was persuaded to return – and the band played on, touring the US and Europe.

*"I think you have too.
Good luck signing on"*

In February 1996, Oasis got revenge on Blur at the Brit Awards – winning three gongs - best group, best video and best album for 'What's the Story Morning Glory'. Oasis didn't disappoint as they collected their awards. Taking one of the awards from the late INXS front man Michael Hutchence, Noel grabbed the mic and announced that, *'Has-beens shouldn't present awards to gonna-bee's.'* Then Liam challenged anyone to come and remove them from the stage, and the group mocked Blur by singing a spoof of their hit 'Parklife'.

As they continued on the road, usual drink-and-drug induced spats between the brothers also continued. However, the tour was notable for its UK summer leg of 1996 which consisted of several open-air concerts to record crowds. The tour included such venues as Maine Road in Manchester – then home to Noel and Liam's beloved Manchester City football team, Loch Lomond in Scotland, Páirc Uí Chaoimh in Ireland and Knebworth Park in England. This fourth venue in particular has gone down in the history of rock and roll. Over two nights in August 1996, the band played to 250,000 people over two nights. Unprecedented for an open-air concert in the UK at the time, the gig also holds the record for the largest ever ticket demand in history with nearly three million (1 in 20 people) ticket applications. The backstage guest list alone had over 7,000 people on it!

"Has-beens shouldn't present awards to gonna-bee's"

MAIN IMAGE: Liam at Knebworth, August 1996
TOP LEFT: Oasis & Michael Hutchence, the Brit Awards, 1996
TOP RIGHT: Poster for the Knebworth live album

"Right here, right now.
This is history."

MAIN IMAGE: Still from the 2021 Jake Scott
documentary, Oasis Knebworth 1996
TOP RIGHT: Knebworth ticket

'This is history, this is history,' yelled a swaggering Noel Gallagher, to a sea of deafening cheers. 'Right here, right now. This is history.'

Oasis' double-header at Maine Road months earlier were arguably better gigs but Knebworth felt like an era defining event. It was so colossal, it was bordering on the ridiculous. Even guitarist Paul 'Bonehead' Arthurs admitted that the band should have quit following their huge outdoor shows, knowing that it really couldn't get any better than this.

And then, of course, there was Oasis' performance itself. In the words of one reviewer...

'Noel and Liam turned up with their chests pumped right out, ready to make a statement of rock 'n' roll intent. Having the balls to kick off their set with a bulldozing rendition of Columbia instead of one of their big hitting stadium anthems was a bold and brilliant move which every die-hard Oasis fan embraced with open arms. Only Rock 'N' Roll Star would have topped it. But sadly, it never even made the final cut. From there on in, it was a non-stop party as Oasis rolled out both hits Roll With It, What's The Story Morning Glory, Wonderwall, Live Forever and Don't Look Back In Anger, and massively underrated B-sides - the anthemic Acquiesce, Noel's majestic 'Masterpla'. They road tested forthcoming Be Here Now tracks My Big Mouth and It's Gettin' Better (Man!!. But they really didn't compare to the jukebox quality of those Morning Glory hits, which had been on repeat in pubs throughout the land for months'.

From these truly lofty heights, the only way was down...

MAIN IMAGE: Still from the 2021 Jake Scott documentary, Oasis Knebworth 1996

chapter 5
BE HERE NOW

'I don't have a bad word to say about Be Here Now. The only person who's got a problem with it is Noel. He wrote it, so then it's his problem'

Liam Gallagher

'Be Here Now – clearly a s**t f**king album, full of fat fucking rock stars'

Noel Gallagher

The dream had come true – bigger and better than they could ever have imagined. Not only had they played to record breaking crowds, What's The Story Morning Glory was well on its way to becoming the third-ever best-selling album by a British band in the UK - topped only by the Beatles' Sgt Pepper's Lonely Hearts Club Band and Queen's Greatest Hits. They were feted and flattered by fans and celebrity followers alike. They were the Kings of Britpop, the champions of the world, and Noel and Liam's fame and charisma jettisoned them into the 'A' list league. Liam was loved-up with uber-babe blonde actress and model Patsy Kensit. They had become Cool Britannia's 'It' couple, photographed together on a union-flag covered bed for the cover of prestigious glossy magazine, 'Vanity Fair'. Noel, meanwhile, was in a serious relationship with PR girl Meg Mathews, and he hung out with the likes of Paul McCartney, U2's Bono, Johnny Depp and Kate Moss. Beneath the glittering 'A' list veneer, however, the old problems remained.

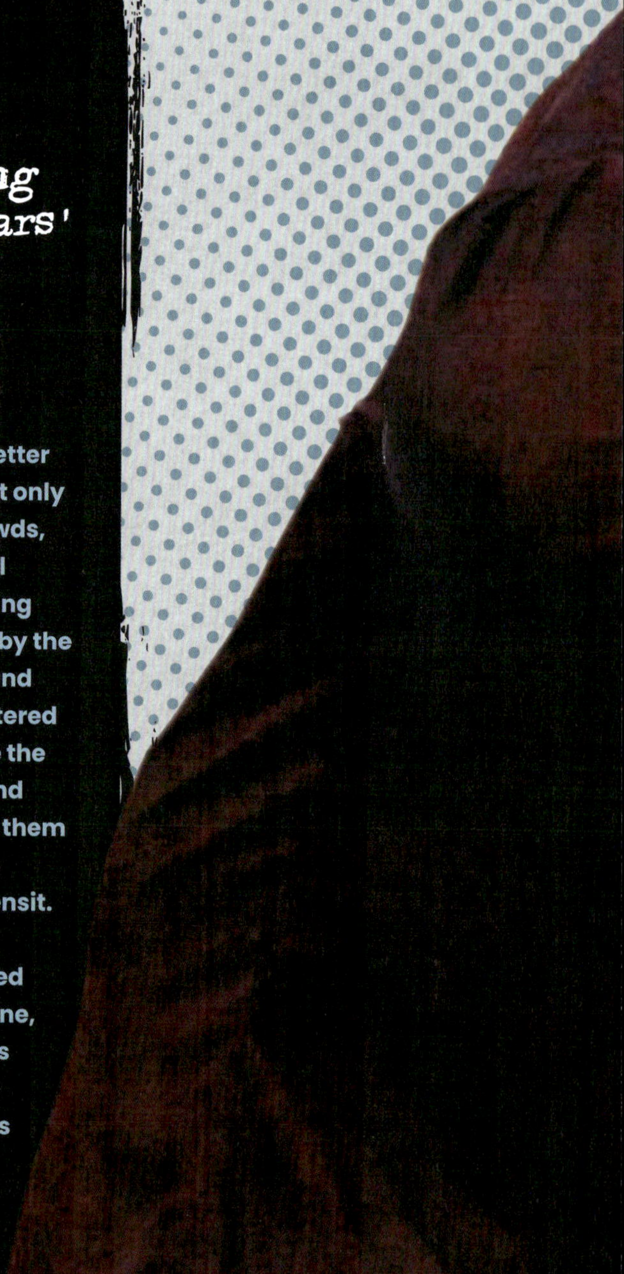

MAIN IMAGE: Liam Gallagher, 1997

MAIN IMAGE: Liam Gallagher with fiancee Patsy Kensit arrive at the first screening of the film The Rolling Stones Rock And Roll Circus at London Astoria

" ...perform for f**king silly yanks"

Shortly after the Knebworth triumph, Liam refused to sing for an MTV Unplugged performance at London's Royal Festival Hall, pleading a sore throat. Though he did attend the concert, he spent the evening heckling Noel from the upper level balcony. Four days later, he refused to participate in the first leg of their American tour, pulling out 15 minutes before the plan was due to take off, claiming he had nowhere to live in the UK and that he must go house-hunting with Patsy.

'We've got to be out by the weekend and I'm not going around touring the US when I've got nowhere to live,' he said. *'I've got to pack my gear and get a home sorted out. I can't go and look at houses while I'm in America trying to perform for f**king silly yanks.'*

He re-joined the band a few days afterwards for a key concert at the MTV Video Music Awards in New York, but intentionally sang out-of-tune and spat beer and saliva during the performance. The following day, a UK tabloid led with the front-page headline *'America sickened by obscene Liam's spitting rampage.'*

Amongst much internal bickering, the tour continued—with Liam— to Charlotte, North Carolina, where Noel finally lost patience with his brother and announced he was leaving the band – again.

He later admitted, *'If the truth be known, I didn't want to be there anyway. I wasn't prepared to be in the band if people were being like that to each other. There was no point in blitzing America. Whatever is meant to happen in this walk of life will happen. Whatever will be will be. Why be in a band if we're all going to end up in the cuckoo farm?'*

The band's management and record company, worried that Oasis would implode and burn themselves out for good if they stayed on the road, suggested they go back into the studio and record another album. It was while Noel and Meg were staying in Mick Jagger's villa on the exclusive Caribbean island of Mustique with Johnny Depp and Kate Moss that he started demoing songs for the third, eagerly anticipated album. The band's producer Owen Morris joined him later on and they recorded demos with a drum machine and a keyboard. But when it came to actually recording the album for real, the demos were not used as much as they might have been.

'I have to say that I cocked up, and I think Noel did too, in not using and referencing the demos more on the actual album sessions,' Morris was later to say. *'Be Here Now would have been a far better record had*

" It's a f**king top laugh "

MAIN IMAGE: Noel Gallagher performing at the 1996 MTV Video Music Awards Show
RIGHT: Ridge Farm Studios in Surrey

we been able to use Noel's guitars and bass and percussion from the Mustique demos. We could've just overdubbed the drums and Liam's singing, and Bonehead's guitar and that would have been a great album. So, I very sadly admit that I mucked up royally there.

The band went into the famous Abbey Road studios in October 1996. To begin with, things went well with Noel commenting, '*I think as soon as we started making the record we just said, "What are we moaning about? It's a f**king top laugh".*' But Morris disagreed, describing the first week as '*f**king awful*', and suggested to Noel that they abandon the session. '*But he just shrugged and said it would be all right. So on we went.*'

It wasn't the best environment – there was too much partying, too many liggers, hangers-on and drug dealers sniffing around. Liam was under heavy tabloid focus at the time, and in November 1996 was arrested and cautioned for cocaine possession following a bender at the *Q* Awards. A media frenzy ensued, and the band's management made the decision to move to a studio less readily accessible to paparazzi. In paranoia, Oasis cut themselves off from their wider circle.

According to Johnny Hopkins, the publicist of Oasis's label Creation Records, '*People were being edged out of the circle around Oasis. People who knew them before they were famous rather than because they were famous.*' Hopkins likened the scenario to a medieval court, complete with kings, courtiers and jesters, explaining, '*once you're in that situation you lose sight of reality.*'

On November 11 1996, Oasis relocated to the rural Ridge Farm Studios in Surrey. Though the band reconvened with more energy, the early recordings were compromised by the drug intake of all involved. Morris recalled that '*in the first week, someone tried to score an ounce of weed, but instead got an ounce of cocaine. Which kind of summed it up.*'

"I just carried on shovelling drugs up my nose"

MAIN IMAGE: Oasis perform at Brabanthallen, Den Bosch, Netherlands 27th November, 1997

Noel was not present during any of Liam's vocal track recordings, typifying the high drama surrounding the sessions. Morris thought that the new material was weak, but when he voiced his opinion to Noel he was cut down.

'So,' said Morris, 'I just carried on shovelling drugs up my nose.'

Noel, wanting to make the album as dense and 'colossal' feeling as possible, layered multiple guitar tracks on several of the songs, dubbing 10 channels with identical guitar parts, in an effort to create a sonic volume.

Alan McGee visited the studio during the mixing stage. 'I used to go down to the studio, and there was so much cocaine getting done at that point ... Owen was out of control, and he was the one in charge of it. The music was just fucking loud.'

Morris' response was, 'Alan McGee was the head of the record company. Why didn't he do something about the "out of control" record producer? Obviously, the one not in control was the head of the record company.'

When McGee, Johnny Hopkins, and marketing executive Emma Greengrass first heard Be Here Now at Noel Gallagher's Primrose Hill mansion, all had doubts about its artistic value but kept these doubts to themselves.

One Creation employee recalled, 'a lot of nodding of heads, a lot of slapping of backs.' McGee later admitted to having strong misgivings at first. 'I heard it in the studio and I remember saying "We'll only sell seven million copies" ... I thought it was too confrontational.'

However, in an interview with the music press a few days later he predicted the album would sell 20 million copies. McGee's prediction alarmed both Oasis and their management company, Ignition, and both immediately excluded him from involvement in the release campaign. Ignition's strategy from that point on centred on an effort to suppress all publicity, and withheld access to both music and information from anybody not directly involved with the album's release. Fearful of the dangers of over-hype and bootlegging, their aim was to present the record as a 'regular, everyday collection of tunes'. To this end they planned a modest marketing budget, to be spent on subdued promotional activities such as street posters and music press adverts, while avoiding billboards and TV advertising.

"The campaign made people despise Oasis"

According to Greengrass, *'We want to keep it low key. We want to keep control of the whole mad thing.'*

The plan backfired. Controlling access to the album generated more hype than could normally have been expected, and served to alienate members of both the print and broadcast media, as well as most of the Creation staff. When D'you Know What I Mean?' was planned as the first single, Ignition decided on a late release to radio so as to avoid too much advance exposure. However, three stations broke the embargo, and Ignition panicked.

According to Greengrass, *'We'd been in these bloody bunker meetings for six months or something, and our plot was blown. It was a nightmare'.* BBC Radio One received a CD containing three songs 10 days before the album's release, on condition that disc jockey Steve Lamacq talked over the tracks to prevent illegal copies being made by listeners. The day after Lamacq previewed the album on his show, he received a phone call from Ignition informing him that he would not be able to preview further tracks because he didn't speak enough over the songs. Lamacq said, *'I had to go on the air the next night and say, "Sorry, but we're not getting any more tracks." It was just absurd.'*

According to Creation's head of marketing John Andrews, *'The campaign made people despise Oasis within Creation. You had this Oasis camp that was like "I'm sorry, you're not allowed come into the office between the following hours. You're not allowed to mention the word Oasis." It was like a fascist state.'* One employee recalled an incident *'when somebody came round to check our phones because they thought The Sun had tapped them.'*

"It was just absurd"

MAIN IMAGE: Oasis portrait, Milan, Italy, 1997
RIGHT: Disc jockey Steve Lamacq

When Hopkins began to circulate cassette copies of the album to the music press a few weeks later, he required each journalist sign a contract containing a clause requiring that the cassette recipient, according to Select journalist Mark Perry, 'not discuss the album with anyone—including your partner at home. It basically said don't talk to your girlfriend about it when you're at home in bed.'

Reflecting in 1999, Greengrass admitted, 'In retrospect a lot of the things we did were ridiculous. We sit in [Oasis] meetings today and we're like "It's on the Internet. It's in Camden Market. Whatever." I think we've learned our lesson.' According to Perry, 'It seemed, particularly once you heard the album, that this was cocaine grandeur of just the most ludicrous degree. I remember listening to All Around the World and laughing—actually quite pleasurably—because it seemed so ridiculous. You just thought, "Christ, there is so much coke being done here".'

As Noel himself testified. When the album was slammed by critics for being 'cocaine set to music', he came back with, 'You should have tried Be Here Now on nine grams of Charlie because that's what it was written on'. Later on, he was to say with regards to following the time-honoured

"... a bunch of guys, on coke, in the studio, not giving a f**k"

song writing formula of taking inspiration from what was around him, *'I tried to do that with Be Here Now and it was all champagne and supermodels. Who wants to hear that when you're on your way to work?'*

Be Here Now was finally released in August 1997 and by the end of the year, had sold eight million units worldwide but buyers had realised that the album was not another Definitely Maybe or What's the Story Morning Glory? The music media, too, began to change tact, despite having initially praised the album.

'So colossally did Be Here Now fall short of expectations that it killed Britpop and ushered in an era of more ambitious, less overblown music,' commented one publication.

'Bloated and over-heated, the album has all that dreadful braggadocio that is so characteristic of a cocaine user,' wrote another.

'The third Oasis album is a loud, lumbering noise signifying nothing,' was another. *'It's the sound of ... a bunch of guys, on coke, in the studio, not giving a f**k. There's no bass to it at all – I don't know what happened to that ... And all the songs are really long and all the lyrics are shit and for every millisecond Liam is not saying a word, there's a f**kin' guitar riff in there in a Wayne's World stylie.'*

'I wish we'd let What's the Story settle and go away,' said Noel in retrospect. *'It was still number 5 in the Billboard 100 when we started making Be Here Now. I wish someone who's paid to be bright and clever had told us to go away and do a bit of living. But we were fuelled by youth and cocaine. Everything was going to be bigger and better. We were surrounded by people telling us it was the greatest thing they'd ever heard. When you're the cash cow, people are always going to cheer you on whatever.'*

As early as July 1997, Noel was 'talking down' Be Here Now in the music press, describing the production as *'bland'* and remarking that some of the tracks were *'f**king shit'*.

Liam, predictably enough, didn't agree and was later to comment, *'At the time we thought it was f**king great, and I still think it's great. It just wasn't Morning Glory. If he (Noel) didn't like the record that much, he shouldn't have put the f**king record out in the first place ... I don't know what's up with him but it's a top record, man, and I'm proud of it—it's just a little bit long.'*

ABOVE LEFT: Be Here Now Vinyl
ABOVE RIGHT: Be Here Now promo poster

ABOVE: Oasis at Westpoint Arena, Exeter, UK, September 1997

"We should work like f**king monkeys. I'm mad for it"

Although Noel had always said that the music was everything and absolutely what he wanted to be known for, by summer 1997 he was becoming famous for schmoozing with the new British Prime Minister, New Labour's Tony Blair. In July 1997, he and Meg, to whom he was now married, attended a music industry reception at 10 Downing Street and were later criticised for it. Both Liam and Blur's Damon Albarn declined their invitations, with Albarn commenting, *'Enjoy the schmooze, comrade'*. The perception of Noel Gallagher as someone now mixing with politicians— illustrated, in particular, by a famous photograph of him sipping champagne with Blair—conflicted with the 'working class hero' status.

Liam, too, had things other than the band on his mind. In April '97, he married Pasty, supposedly putting his wild, womanising days behind him.

'It finally happened at Marylebone Registry Office. Half seven in the morning in my jeans. It was top. Me, Pats, the builder who's doing my house and her hairdresser. Just kept it small really, otherwise we were never going to get it done. And we thought, if we go on honeymoon everyone's going to follow us so there's no point. We reckoned we'd leave it for a bit. That was it: just stayed in the hotel for three days and got off it. Like you do. It (marriage) has not mellowed me, it's just made me feel more important 'cos someone wants to spend the rest of her life with me – that's nice.'

Noel may not have been happy with Be Here Now but what was done was done. It was time to get back on the road but a joint interview with him and Liam – their first since 1994 – gave some insight into their respective states of mind.

'I don't think we should ever have time off again,' said Liam. *'We should work like f**king monkeys. I'm mad for it!'*

Noel's appraisal couldn't have been more different.

'Work's become boring,' said Noel. *'Everything that led up to Knebworth was really special but now we've just become another band. It's sort of not exciting anymore. Mentally, I need time off.'*

But that's not what he was going to get. . .

]

ABOVE & RIGHT: Oasis perform on stage at The National Indoor Arena during the 'Be Here Now' tour, on September 30th, 1997 in Birmingham, England

chapter 6
POST BRIT POP

'The good years were from '91 to Knebworth. Then it levelled out. There was nowhere else to go. What do you do? It was the apex and then we made the mistake of coming off stage and going to America for six weeks when we should have come off stage at Knebworth and disappeared'

Noel Gallagher

oasis

BE HERE NOW

November

3rd – France; Lille, Zenith
4th – France; Paris, Bercy
6th – France; Angers, Parc des Expositions
7th – France; Bordeaux, Patinoire
8th – Spain; Zaragoza, Pabellon Principe Felipe
10th – Spain; Madrid, Palacio de la Comunidad
11th – Spain; Barcelona, Palau Dels Esports
13th – Switzerland; Geneva, Arena
15th – Italy; Bologna, Palasport
16th – Italy; Milan, Forum
17th – Italy; Milan, Forum
19th – Germany; Munich, Olympichalle
21st – Czech Republic; Prague, Sportovni Hall
22nd – Germany; Berlin, Deutschlandhalle
24th – Germany; Hannover, Messehalle
25th – Germany; Frankfurt, Festhalle
27th – Holland; Den Bosch, Brabanthallen
28th – Germany; Oberhausen, Arena

December

4th – Eire; Dublin, Point Depot
5th – Eire; Dublin, Point Depot
7th – UK; Glasgow, SE & CC
8th – UK; Glasgow, SE & CC
10th – UK; Cardiff, Cardiff Indoor Arena
11th – UK; Cardiff, Cardiff Indoor Arena
13th – UK; Manchester, GMEX
14th – UK; Manchester, GMEX
16th – UK; London, Wembley Arena
17th – UK; London, Wembley Arena
18th – UK; London, Wembley Arena

Live 1997

nstead of taking time out, it was straight back into the studio after Oasis had toured Be Here Now. They started making Standing on the Shoulder of Giants in 1999 in a studio in the South of France. Tensions were high but inspiration on song writer Noel's part extremely low. It was to be an extremely fraught recording.

'We should have never made Standing on the Shoulder of Giants,' Gallagher was to say of the 2000 release. 'I'd come to the end. At the time, I had no reason or desire to make music. I had no drive. We'd sold all these f**king records and there just seemed to be no point. Liam, to his credit, was the one who was like, "We're going to make a record, we're going into the studio next month, and you better have some f**king songs written". We should have gone to wherever it is the Rolling Stones disappear to, wherever the f**k that is. Rent a boat and sail around the Bahamas or whatever. But I went ahead and did it, even though I had no inspiration and couldn't find inspiration anywhere. I just wrote songs for the sake of making an album. We needed a reason to go on a tour. But at the time, I wasn't thinking like that. It's the only album I've written while I was straight.'

MAIN IMAGE: Noel Gallagher, 1999
LEFT: Be Here Now tour poster

By now Noel had stopped taking drugs and also cut back on drinking. In 1998, he had returned from tour to his and Meg's home, 'Supernova Heights' in trendy Primrose Hill, north London, to find it full of people he didn't know who had transformed the house into a nightclub. He later remarked, *'I'm not having that – I need to get a f***in' life and I never touched cocaine again. But to get off it I had to go on prescription drugs, which is f**king worse because they come from a doctor. It's just uppers and downers that replace the cocaine and booze. I wanted to change my life. I was getting frustrated. I'd made this big decision in my life to kick these drugs. I wanted to get my head straight.'*

It didn't help that Noel was trying to keep Liam clean.

'We went to France to record because we were trying to get Liam off the drink,' he was later to say. *'It makes recording a really difficult thing to do when he's pissed. So I said, "No one can drink while we're there because it won't be fair on Liam". I said I would kick it in the head for three months. We needed to give him all the support we could – everyone agreed to lay off it. But Bonehead would go off on the piss. I said, "You're just rubbing it in his face – if I'm not drinking then no c**t is. So we'd all be there drinking water and Bonehead would be knocking back red wine. I politely asked him to give it a rest and he told me to f**k off. Then there was an argument.'*

There was also a departure. Bonehead decided to leave the band – but not just because Noel said he couldn't drink.

'The original spark didn't feel like it was there, it really didn't,' he said. *'I don't know, it had just gone. I just thought I can't go on with this, to sort of kid people I'm giving it my all when I won't be so I just made my decision, that was the main reason.'*

With Bonehead gone, Guigsy decided he'd had enough, too. An official statement issued by the band's label announced Guigsy's departure a few weeks later.

'Paul has finished his work on the recordings of the new album and feels now is an opportune time to leave before the band undertakes touring and promotional activities later on this year.'

'We've been left holding the sh**e sandwich,' drawled Noel, at a press conference in a dingy back room of the Water Rats pub near London's

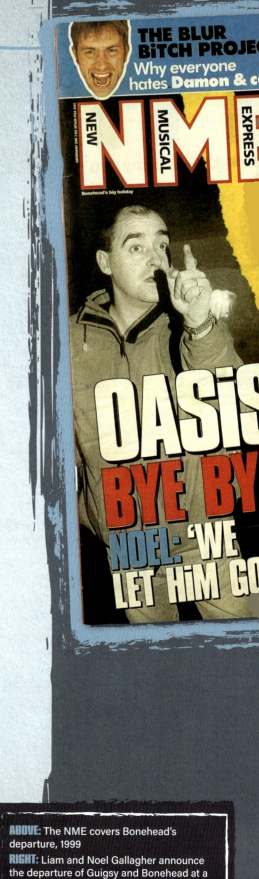

ABOVE: The NME covers Bonehead's departure, 1999

RIGHT: Liam and Noel Gallagher announce the departure of Guigsy and Bonehead at a press conference held in The Water Rats pub in London, August 25, 1999

'KELLY'S HUNG
LIKE A MOUSE'
Stereophonics answer
your probing questions

14 AUGUST 1999 £1.15 S(US)4.75
http://www.nme.com

XCLUSiVE
BONEHEAD

9 770028 636116   32>

"We've been left holding the sh**e sandwich"

King's Cross, where the band had played their first London concert. *'Yeah, we're shocked but we have to get the album out and tour.'* With reference to Guisgy he added, somewhat uncharitably, *'It's hardly Paul McCartney leaving The Beatles.'* This was quite to contrast to how he'd viewed Guigsy four years earlier when the bass player had taken time out. Then he'd said, *'Guigsy is Oasis – if he leaves, the band is finished.'*

Liam couldn't hide his upset.

*'I felt hurt. 'Cos we'd been in it so long I thought we were that f**king close. When we were together, the band, we talked about things. If I had a problem with the band, I'd say it. If Noel did, and if Whitey did, they'd say it. And I just feel a bit gutted that Bonehead and Guigsy mustn't have felt like we were mates or something, that they couldn't come out and go, "Oh I've got a problem".'*

TOP LEFT: Andy Bell

RIGHT: Gem Archer with Noel Gallagher

TOP RIGHT: NME covering the end of Creation

LEFT: Standing on the Shoulder of Giants cover

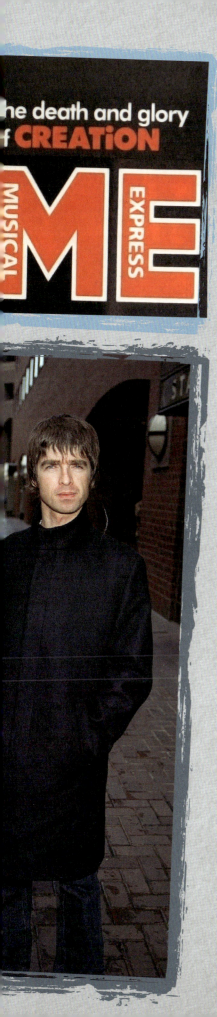

"up there with some of the best things that I've done"

The now three-piece Oasis chose to continue recording the album, with Noel re-recording most of Arthurs' guitar and McGuigan's bass parts. After the completion of the recording sessions, the band began searching for replacement members. The first new member to be announced was new lead/rhythm guitarist Colin 'Gem' Archer, formerly of Heavy Stereo, who later claimed to have been approached by Noel Gallagher only a couple of days after Arthurs' departure was publicly announced. Finding a replacement bassist took more time and effort. Finally they brought in Andy Bell, former guitarist/songwriter of Ride and Hurricane No. 1 as their new bassist. Bell had never played bass before and had to learn to play it. Liam felt this wouldn't be a problem. *'If he can play the guitar, he can play the f**kin' bass,'* he said.

But another problem arose when Alan McGee decided to fold Creation Records. As a result, Oasis formed their own label, 'Big Brother' which released all of Oasis' subsequent records in the UK and Ireland.

'Standing on the Shoulder of Giants' was released in February 2000 to good first-week sales. It peaked at number one on the British charts and number 24 on the Billboard charts. Three singles were released from the album – Go Let It Out, Who Feels Love and Sunday Morning Call, all of which were top five UK singles. The Go Let It Out video was shot before Bell joined the group and therefore featured the unusual line-up of Liam on rhythm guitar, Archer on lead guitar and Noel on bass.

With the departure of the founding members, the band made several small changes to their image and sound. The cover featured a new Oasis logo, designed by Gem Archer, and the album was also the first Oasis release to include a song written by Liam Gallagher, entitled Little James, about Patsy Kensit's son from her previous marriage to Simple Minds vocalist, Jim Kerr. The songs also had more experimental, psychedelic influences. However, Standing on the Shoulder of Giants received only lukewarm reviews and became the band's lowest selling studio album. nevertheless, Noel Gallagher has stated that he regards Go Let It Out as being ,*'up there with some of the best things that I've done.'*

To support the album, the band staged a world tour which turned out to be highly eventful for all the wrong reasons. While playing in Barcelona in May 2000, Oasis were forced to cancel a gig when an attack of tendonitis caused Alan White's arm to seize up, and the Gallaghers spent the evening binge drinking instead. As the night wore on, an argument broke out in which Liam allegedly questioned the paternity of Noel's baby daughter, Anaïs, with the result that Noel attacked his brother.

"If you're going to carry on with the tour, you do it without me"

'I lost it with him,' Noel was later to say. *'It was a proper fight – it wasn't like, "I'll scratch your eyes out, you bitch!" It was a proper brawl and I'm actually quite proud of the fact that it came to blows. He knew if he crossed me I'd leave him in the shit.'*

That's just what Noel did. He left the band - again - mid-tour.

'Liam hurt me pretty fucking badly, emotionally,' he said. *'The only way to get at him was, "If you're going to carry on with the tour, you do it without me".'*

Oasis completed the remaining European dates without Noel – Mother Earth guitarist Matt Deighton deputising for some gigs. Noel declared he was quitting touring overseas altogether but eventually returned for the Irish and British legs of the tour, which included two major shows at Wembley Stadium.

On a personal level, life was not good, either. By early 2001 Noel and Meg's marriage was over, despite becoming parents only eight months earlier. A statement read. . .

'They have simply drifted apart over the last year or so. Their relationship started when Oasis were still in their infancy, and the couple have been together through the whole meteoric rise of the band, and the turbulent years that followed, always under the constant glare of the media. Many things have changed in that time, including themselves it seems.'

Noel himself was more specific.

'For about a year leading up to Meg getting pregnant I was thinking, "This ain't going to work". Then Meg got pregnant and it was OK. But after that it went pear-shaped getting back to the way it was, the constant larging it. I just couldn't be doing with it any more.'

As for Liam? His marriage to Patsy Kensit had broken down in 2000, shortly after the birth of their son, Lennon. It transpires Liam had been unfaithful, conducting a two year on-off affair with singer/songwriter Lisa Moorish, which had resulted in the birth of a daughter, Molly, in March 1998. In true Liam style, during the 'Standing on the Shoulder of Giants' tour, he would regale fans with his domestic problems between songs.

ABOVE: Liam Gallagher plays to a sell out crowd at the Universal Amphitheatre, Universal City, California, September 2000

'If you think I'm over the moon to be here you must be tripping. Patsy's gone and taken the furniture with the solicitors. I don't even have a teabag to my name. I was forced into it. No, it wasn't an arranged marriage, it was more a deranged marriage.'

There were compensations, though. Now Noel was no longer with Meg nor Liam with Patsy, the brothers' relationship became easier.

'As soon as Noel got divorced from his missus and as soon as I got divorced, we got on better. It wasn't just those two (ie, Patsy and Meg), it was their crowd. They're a bunch of parasites,' said Liam

They even got to play happy families with new girlfriends – Noel was now with PR girl Sara McDonald while Liam was seeing All Saints' Nicole Appleton.

"They 're a bunch of parasites"

'So now that Liam's with Nicky and I'm with Sara, we got out in a foursome for Sunday lunch and stuff like that,' said Noel in 2001. *'And we have the funniest, funniest times, which we never did before. I don't know if it is a cliché or not but behind these two very happy brothers are two very good ladies.'*

Not that the 'Happy Families' truce lasted long. The band's fifth studio album 'Heathen Chemistry' was recorded during 2001 and early 2002, and is the first Oasis album to have significant writing contributions from members other than Noel. Liam contributed three songs, while new bassist Andy Bell and lead guitarist Gem Archer contributed one each. Although most of the song's instrumentation was complete by mid-to-late 2001, Noel indicated that the release date of the album was being needlessly delayed by Liam's apparent reluctance to lay down his vocal parts at recording sessions, and went on to state that he was *'livid'* at the lack of work being done.

'I was really happy with (the album) until recently, but I'm f**king livid now. It was drawn-out, painful process. So, to be honest with you, I don't know when it'll come out now. It's down to him (Liam). I finished my bits three-and-a-half months ago, and then we handed it over to Liam, and in three-and-a-half months he's done nothing. Just concentrated on his drinking habit again. It's just drifting at the moment. All the backing tracks are done and it's a fantastic album of instrumentals. Hand it over to the singer and it just slows down.'

MAIN IMAGE: Noel Gallagher performs with Oasis at the Chicago Theater in Chicago, Illinois, April 27, 2000

TOP LEFT: Noel and Liam Gallagher, brotherly love, on stage at Glasgow Green Festival, August 2000

ABOVE: Oasis play a secret gig at Shepherd's Bush Empire, West London in front of 400 people, 2001

"Liam's got his teeth back for Christmas and we're back in business"

Despite the setbacks during the recording process, when the album was finally complete Noel was confident that it was the group's second-best album to date, behind their debut, Definitely Maybe. The title of the album, according to Noel, came from a T-shirt he bought in Ibiza which featured a logo reading, The Society of Heathen Chemists. Similarly, the name of the first single, The Hindu Times, originated from a logo on a T-shirt which Noel saw during a photo shoot for GQ's 100 Greatest Guitarists edition. The name was given to the track when it was just an instrumental and stuck once the track was finished.

There were four singles released from the album – The Hindu Times, Stop Crying Your Heart Out, Little By Little, She is Love which were written by Noel, and Songbird, written by Liam – this was the first single not to be penned by Noel. The record blended the band's sonic experiments from their last albums, but also went for a more basic rock sound. The recording of Heathen Chemistry was much more balanced for the band, with all of the members, apart from White, writing songs. Johnny Marr provided additional guitar as well as backup vocals on a couple of songs. The album Heathen Chemistry reached Number One in the UK and 23 in the US, although critics gave it mixed reviews. The following in 'Rolling Stone' magazine was typical. . .

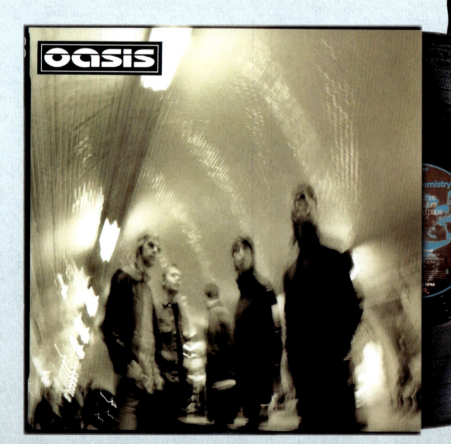

'On the uneven Heathen Chemistry, Noel Gallagher seeks transcendence through a pummelling and thoroughly transfixing T. Rex grind (The Hindu Times, a magnificent drone) but then can't resist a softheaded power ballad (Stop Crying Your Heart Out). His most rousing tune, the U2-ish (Probably) All in the Mind, reconfigures the twelve-bar blues into a metaphysical meditation, while his most contrived offering, Little by Little, is the kind of earnest Wind Beneath My Wings crap even Bryan Adams would know to edit.

As on the last few Oasis outings, particularly the arrogant Standing on the Shoulder of Giants, from 2000, Noel's nerdy-architect tendencies are counterbalanced by the bratty and hedonistic snarl of his brother Liam, who delivers lines such as, "Talking to myself again/This time I think I'm getting through," with a blend of disconsolate moping and simmering, self-loathing frustration he should consider patenting. Liam wrote several songs - the overweening Songbird, the inspired neo-psychedelic fantasy Born on a Different Cloud - but it's his torn-apart vocals that redeem the better material on Chemistry, providing the blood and the guts, the heathen-ness and humanness necessary to make the songs feel like declarations from the heart, not idle exercises.'

After the album's release, the band embarked on a world tour which was once again filled with incident. In late summer 2002, whilst the band were on tour in the US, Noel, Bell and touring keyboardist Jay Darlington were involved in a car accident in Indianapolis. While none of the band members sustained any major injuries, some shows were cancelled as a result. The band's Heathen Chemistry tour was also marred by problems with Liam's voice - a show in Spain in July was postponed and a show in Florida the following month saw the singer leave the stage after four songs. At a show in Fukuoka Kokusai Centre in Japan on October 1, Liam lasted just six songs. In December 2002, the latter half of the German leg of the band's European tour had to be postponed after Liam, Whitey and three other members of the band's entourage were arrested after a violent brawl at a Munich nightclub. The band had been drinking heavily and tests showed that Liam had used cocaine. Liam lost two front teeth and kicked a police officer in the ribs, while Whitey suffered minor head injuries after getting hit with an ashtray.

'All I'm bothered about is that Liam can still sing,' commented Noel. *'Liam's got his teeth back for Christmas and we're back in business.'*

MAIN IMAGE: Oasis at the Fiddler's Green in Englewood, Colorado on May 17, 2001
LEFT: Heathen Chemistry Vinyl cover

The band finished their tour in March 2003 after returning to those postponed dates. But, in retrospect, it was the beginning of the end. . .

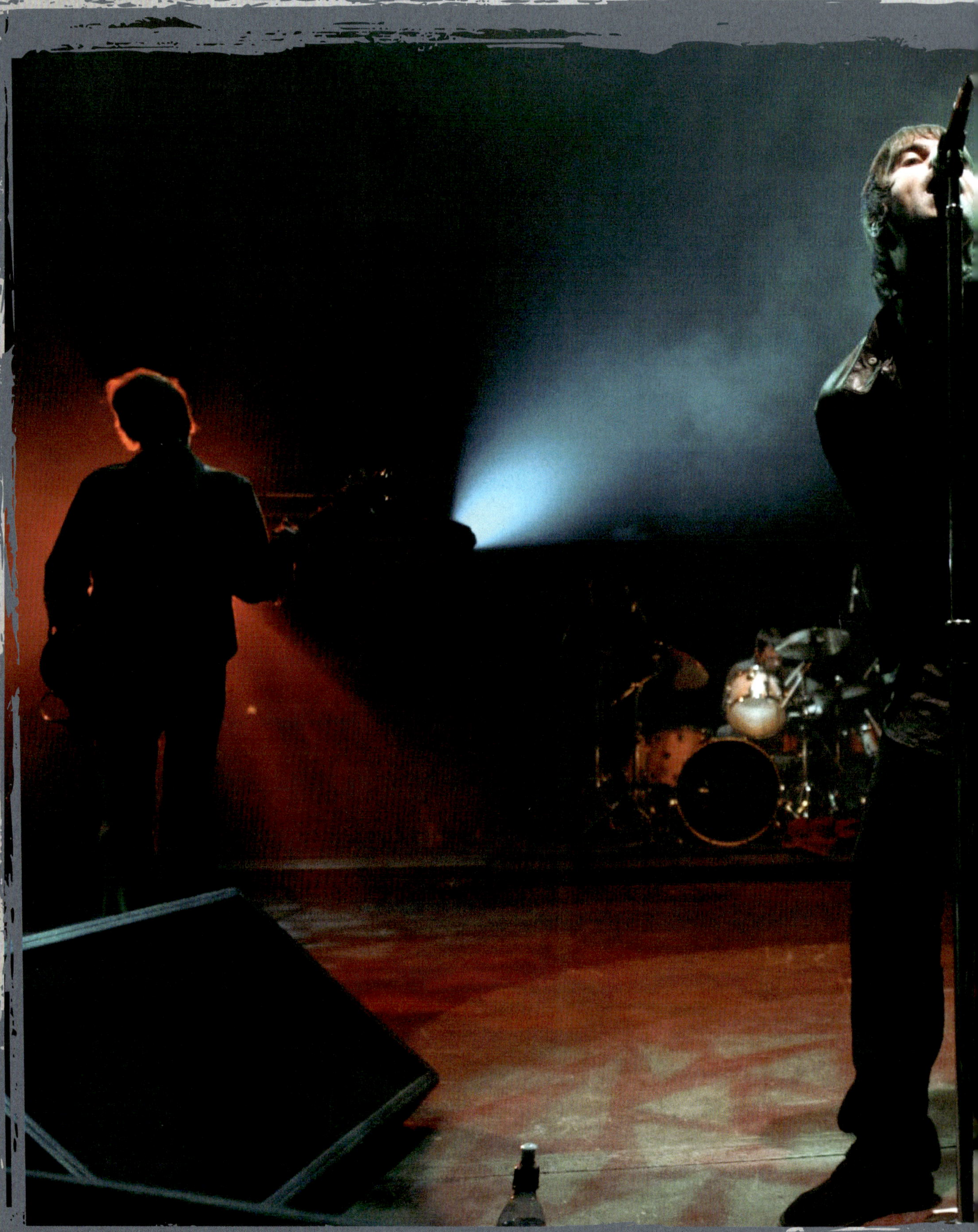

ABOVE: Oasis performing for the "Teenage Cancer Trust" concert at Royal Albert Hall in London, England. February 6, 2002

chapter 7
FAMILY AT WAR

'We're not mates. We just don't feel like it. We get on better when we don't see each other and don't speak to each other so let's not be mates'
Liam Gallagher

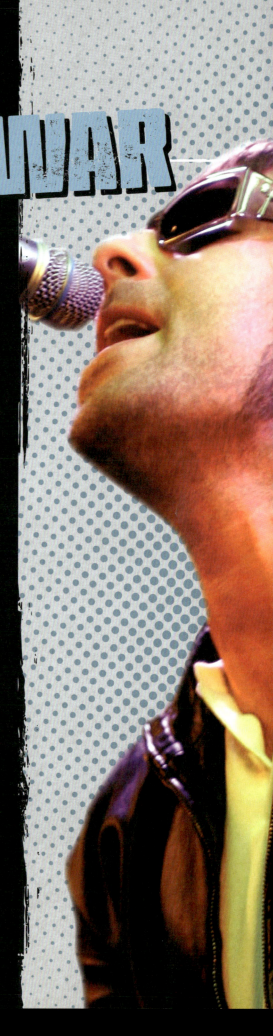

n Oasis tradition, the recording of the band's sixth album, Don't Believe the Truth, was a far from straight-forward process. The album was originally planned for a September 2004 release, to coincide with the 10th anniversary of the release of Definitely Maybe. However, long-time drummer Alan White, who by now had played on nearly all of the band's material, left – or rather was told he was leaving – in late December 2003.

'The bottom line is that Alan got a call four days before Christmas from "The Manager", and he was told he was out of the band,' recounted his brother Steve. *'And he hasn't seen or heard from Noel or Liam since. All Alan wanted, was to have a pint of Stella, and the guys to say what we want is to get Zak Starkey in, as we don't think you're right for us anymore. Alan would have had no problem with that, as nothing lasts forever. But it was just the circumstances of the events which were shocking. The spirit of being in a band was kicked out of him. They shocked me and they hurt Alan.'*

An official Oasis statement read, *'Alan White has been asked to leave Oasis by the other band members. The band's scheduled recording sessions remain unaffected.'*

Zak Starkey, drummer son of Ringo Starr, was Whitey's replacement.

ABOVE: Liam and Noel Gallagher play live, 2005

ABOVE: Oasis perform live on stage during the Glastonbury Festival, June 24, 2004

"We were trying to polish a turd" ——

'We've known Zak for a while and we asked him if he'd play on a few songs and he said yeah, and he has done and it's been absolutely fantastic,' said Noel.

Perhaps. . . but the recordings themselves, produced by Death in Vegas duo Richard Fearless and Tim Holmes, were definitely not. The band were not satisfied with the results.

'Unfortunately, after the recording process we decided we didn't like anything we had played or recorded during those three weeks, and because of commitments with Death in Vegas, Richard Fearless and Tim Holmes couldn't find any more time to give to the project,' announced Noel.

Noel has since commented on numerous occasions that there was no problem with the work done by Death in Vegas, but he felt the songs they were working on were simply not good enough to be included on an album and felt a break was needed in which new material would have to be written. In Noel's words, *'We were trying to polish a turd'.* Around 10 songs were worked on with Death in Vegas of which, according to Noel, six were *'not even good enough to make the B-sides'.* Four of the tracks which eventually appeared on the album had been worked on with Death in Vegas, these being - Turn Up the Sun, Mucky Fingers, A Bell Will Ring and The Meaning of Soul, although all these songs needed extra work or were re-recorded before release.

After a short break in which many new songs, including Let There Be Love, Lyla and Part of the Queue were written, the band reconvened at Wheeler End Studios with Noel as producer. In June 2004, Oasis debuted two new songs from these sessions - the Liam-written The Meaning of Soul, and the Gem-penned A Bell Will Ring - at a live show in Poole, Dorset. A few days later, Oasis headlined the Glastonbury Festival for the second time in their career and performed a mostly 'greatest hits' set. The performance received negative reviews, with NME calling it a *'disaster'.* The BBC's Tom Bishop called Oasis' set *'lacklustre and uneventful ... prompting a mixed reception from fans',* mainly because of Liam's uninspired singing and Starkey's lack of experience with the band's material.

After hearing of the band's production problems from Oasis manager Marcus Russell, American producer Dave Sardy expressed interest in taking over production duties from Noel. Sardy was given tapes of existing recording sessions to mix, and after his work was praised by the band, he arrived in the UK to oversee new recording sessions at Olympic

"I'm tired of people asking if he's in the band"

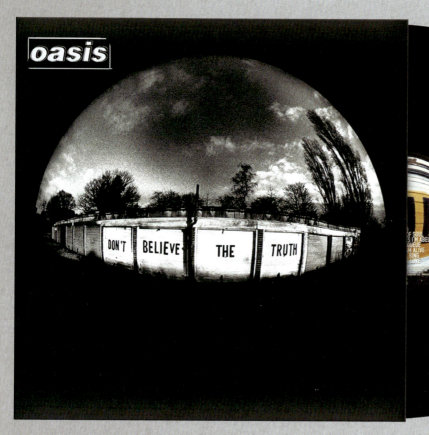

Studios in London. These sessions did not last long before he asked the band to travel to Los Angeles and re-record most of the album there, as he felt more comfortable working in a studio closer to home. With the band eventually agreeing to this, recording sessions began at Capitol Studios in November 2004 with them spending around nine weeks there. Of the 11 songs recorded, five were Noel's, three Liam's, two Andy Bell's and one Gem Archer's – thus making Noel the leader of the band merely on a first-past-the-post basis.

Don't Believe the Truth received generally positive reviews and was considered a return to form for Oasis. Rolling Stone magazine declared it, *'the first Oasis album in years that doesn't sound like a pale self-imitation'* and went on to praise *'its increased emphasis on texture – including plenty of subdued psych-rock atmosphere'.* However, there were some sly digs about Zak Starkey and the Fab Four connection which Noel responded to in his own inimitable way.

'I'm tired of people asking if he's in the band just because his dad was in the Beatles. That would be like getting Stella McCartney to do backing vocals. It'd be fucking ridiculous, wouldn't it!'

ABOVE LEFT: Don't Believe the Truth Vinyl
ABOVE: Don't Believe the Truth promo poster
RIGHT: Oasis Presented With The Most Successful Artist Of The Last Decade By The Book Of British Hit Singles And Albums, May 22, 2005

So, after the release of Don't Believe the Truth, it appeared Oasis had been restored to their former (Morning) glory - two number one singles, a top album chart spot, a handful of awards, and a lengthy world tour which started in May 2005 to promote the album. Over the next 10 months, the band played to more than three million people worldwide. Some of their notable performances were at Madison Square Garden, Milton Keynes Bowl, City of Manchester Stadium, Red Rocks Amphitheatre and the Hollywood Bowl. For once, the tour seemed to be without serious incident.

'This is the longest time I've spent in America without anything going tits-up, which is incredible,' announced Noel, halfway through.

"I can read him and I can f**king play him..."

MAIN IMAGE : Liam Gallagher performs on stage at the third and final day of Heineken Jamming Festival 2005
RIGHT: Dig Out Your Soul cover
ABOVE: Dig Out Your Soul promo poster

However, the Gallagher Brothers' relationship was still problematic with Noel admitting in an interview that he resorted to mental manipulation to get Liam to do what he wanted. *'I've kind of learnt that instead of arguing stuff out with him and ending up in a fight, I work on his psychology and he's completely freaked out by me now. I can read him and I can f**king play him like a slightly disused arcade game.'*

In summer 2007, Oasis started recording their seventh and final album, Dig Out Your Soul.

'For the next record, I really fancy doing a record where we just throw the kitchen sink at it,' Noel said at the time. *'We haven't done that since Be Here Now. I think since Standing on the Shoulder of Giants, we've been trying to prove a point of just bass, drums, guitar and vocals and nothing fancy. But I kind of like fancy.'*

Six songs on the album were written by Noel, three from Liam and one each from Archer and Bell.

'We all write separately and none of us kinda discuss what we're writing because that would be ridiculous,' Noel commented.

ABOVE: Noel Gallagher performs during Oasis' North American Tour at Shoreline Ampitheatre in Mountain View California on September 11, 2005

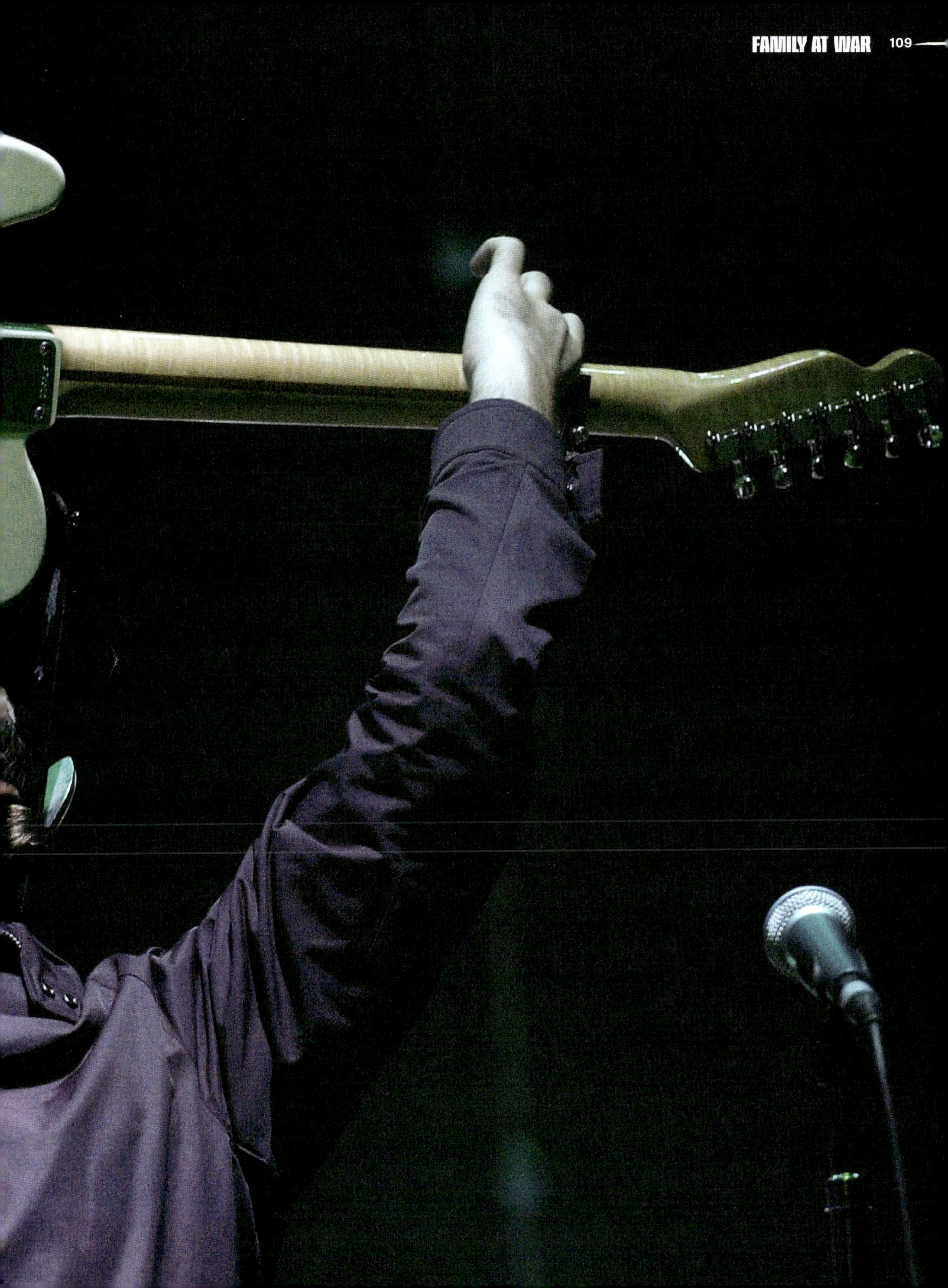

"He's like a man with a fork in a world of soup..."

Inevitably there were problems. During the period when Liam should have been recording his vocals in February 2008, he jetted back from LA to London in order to marry Natalie Appleton. It's said he failed to inform his brother or any of his bandmates of this. Once the album was released – generally positive reviews such as the Observer's *'You could say that if Definitely Maybe was their Stone Roses, Dig Out Your Soul is their Second Coming. It won't win them any new fans, but those that believed the truth last time will dig this'* – there were arguments about who should replace Zak Starkey who had decided to leave in May in order to join The Who on their world tour.

'Liam thought we should get some 16-year-old in. I was like, "You're ludicrous – I'm f**king 40. I'm not playing in a band with some f**king kid who's going to be marauding through the first class lounge throwing heroin everywhere.'

Noel won the day, signing up veteran drummer, Chris Sharrock, to tour the album. As they went back on the road, tensions started to rise. In an interview with Q magazine, Noel made his now legendary comment about Liam. *'He's the angriest man you'll ever meet. He's like a man with a fork in a world of soup'*. That summer saw much bickering between the brothers on social media, with Noel claiming that, *'Life would be easier without Oasis. . .'*

As a result of Liam suffering from laryngitis in August 2009, Oasis cancelled a gig at V Festival in Chelmsford on the 23rd. Noel put out a statement claiming the gig was cancelled due to Liam having *'a hangover'*. Liam then sued Noel for lying and demanded an apology, stating, *'I want Oasis fans, and others who were at V, to know the truth. The truth is I had laryngitis, which Noel was made fully aware of that morning, diagnosed by a doctor.'* Noel later issued an apology and the lawsuit was dropped. But tensions continued to build. A fight between them in a backstage area in late August 2009 reportedly resulted in Liam wielding Noel's guitar like an axe. The group's manager announced the cancellation of their concert at the Rock en Seine festival near Paris just minutes before it was about to begin, along with the cancellation of the last date at I-Day Festival and a statement that the group *'does not exist anymore'*. Two hours later, a statement from Noel appeared on the band's website. . .

'It is with some sadness and great relief...I quit Oasis tonight. People will write and say what they like, but I simply could not go on working with Liam a day longer.'

ABOVE: Chris Sharrock of Oasis performs on stage at the Heineken Music Hall on January 21st 2009 in Amsterdam, Netherlands

A few days later, he elaborated. . .

'Dearly beloved, it is with a heavy heart and a sad face that I say to you this morning. As of last Friday, August 28, I have been forced to leave the Manchester rock n roll pop group, Oasis. The details are not important and of too great a number to list. But I feel you have the right to know that the level of verbal and violent intimidation towards me, my family, friends and comrades has become intolerable. And the lack of support and understanding from my management and band mates has left me with no other option than to get me cape and seek pastures new. I would firstly like to offer my apologies to them kids in Paris who'd paid money and waited all day to see us only to be let down AGAIN by the band. Apologies are not enough, I know, but I'm afraid it's all I've got. While I'm on the subject, I'd like to say to the good people of V Festival that experienced the same thing. Again, I can only apologise – although I don't know why, it was nothing to do with me. I was match fit and ready to be brilliant. Alas, other people in the group weren't up to it. In closing I would like to thank all the Oasis fans, all over the world. The last 18 years have been truly, truly amazing (and I hate that word but today is the one time I'll deem it appropriate). A dream come true. I take with me glorious memories. Now, if you'll excuse me I have a family and a football team to indulge. I'll see you somewhere down the road. It's been a pleasure. Thanks very much. Goodbye.'

Noel was later to reveal that the last six months of Oasis were *'awful'*, *'excruciating'*, and that he and Liam had had a big fight even before starting the Dig Out Your Soul tour.

*'Me and Liam had a massive, massive, massive fistfight three weeks before the world tour started, and fights like that in the past would always be easy to rectify but for some reason I wasn't going to let it go this time. I was just like, "F**k this ****". And there was an atmosphere all the way around the world. By that stage I was flying separately to the rest of the band, which I have to tell you was f**king great. And Liam was sacking tour managers because he didn't like their shoes. Then he starts his own clothing label and starts dedicating songs to it on stage and I'm like, "Really, is this what it's come to?" He's modelling parkas on stage which you could buy on his website. And it's just like, "This is not for me". All that being said, we had two gigs left and I reckon if I'd had got to the end of that tour and I'd had six months off I would have just forgotten about it, got on with it. But the straw that broke the camel's back was the night in Paris and that was a fight. There's no hidden darkness. It was just a fight about f***ing nonsense,*

"It's been a pleasure.
Thanks very much. Goodbye"

ABOVE: Noel Gallagher, 2010

"He's like a man with a fork
in a world of soup..."

just him being p***ed. He'd cancelled the gig at the V Festival and we were getting loads of s**t for it ... He'd gone into his private dressing room and he'd picked up this guitar. He came back in and he was wielding it about like an axe. He was quite violent. At that point, there was no physical violence but there was a lot of World Wrestling Federation stuff. It was an unnecessarily violent act and he nearly took my face off. Liam's convinced I'm some kind of puppet-master, and he blames it all on me. And then it just escalated. It blew up. And that was it. I sat in the car and thought, 'You know what, I've done enough now. F**k it, I'm going to leave' ... If I'd thought there was anything left to achieve I wouldn't have left Oasis ... You name it, we did it all.'

Liam argues that he was provoked, 'He set a few booby traps for me, and I walked right into them because I'm passionate and I wear my heart on my sleeve', that Noel had been secretly planning to leave the band for months or even years and that Noel's accounts of an attempted assault with a guitar are false. 'They tried to treat me like some kind of f**king drummer or hired hand. I'm the f**king face of the band! I'm the voice of the band, and that goes a long f**king way.'

But there was no band left. Oasis were no more. . .

ABOVE: Liam Gallagher performing in Berlin, 2009

chapter 8
SEPARATE LIVES

'Oasis are done, this is something new'
Liam Gallagher

Liam totally blamed Noel for the split.

'He's a sh**bag,' he raged in one interview. 'He wormed his way through that band and used people and sacked people and then f**ked us all off at the end for him to further his f**king sh***y little cosmic pop career. Sacked the f**king drummer, made it impossible for Bonehead to be in the band, Guigsy left after, Whitey went. But it still weren't enough. But he didn't have the b*****ks to sack me. One minute I'm there, next minute I'm under the bus, like some f**king drummer. F**k that, I'm Liam f**king Gallagher, I sang my b***s off, I'm the voice of that band, and now you want me to just f**king disappear and have a little laugh about it? I don't f**king think so, mate. I see you in Marylebone, I see you f**king out, you'd better have a f**king security guard with you and you'd better be paying him good money, because you'd better f**king run, mate. That's how pissed off I am, man, completely.'

Liam didn't rest on his laurels. Immediately after the 'split-gate' gig, he and the other members of Oasis decided to carry on.

'There was no crying or weeping or anything,' he recalled. 'We all wanted to carry on, and stay on our musical journey, you know what I mean? We decided to meet up in November, and have a crack at making some demos or whatever. We couldn't wait that long, so we met up the following week and got cracking.'

Three months later Liam announce he was starting a new band called Beady Eye with former Oasis' members Gem Archer, Andy Bell and Chris Sharrock. They'd written new material and planned to start gigging shortly.

ABOVE: Liam Gallagher performs at Etihad Stadium, Manchester, England, June 1 2022

"It's exciting to start
something new"

'We've been demo-ing some songs that we've had for a bit. Just doing that, on the quiet, not making a big fuss about it,' he told MTV in November 2009. 'After Christmas, we might go in the studio and record them and hopefully have an album out in July. I'll try and reconnect with a new band, new songs, and I'm feeling confident about the songs. I'm feeling a million percent confident that they could be better than Oasis.'

Beady Eye's first album, Different Gear, Still Speeding, was released in February 2011.

'It's exciting to start something new,' said Liam in an interview. 'That's what we gotta do, you know what I mean? It was forced upon us. You don't just stop making music because Noel Gallagher leaves the band, you know what I mean? If people think it was all about Noel, they're very wrong. We're all music lovers, we're all into it. Maybe it's good that people have low expectations of us. Beady Eye is different I think it sounds a lot fresher, a lot grander. The playing, the singing, it's got a real zest to it. This couldn't be an Oasis album. It's got a brand new feeling about it.'

ABOVE: Liam Gallagher and Beady Eye on TV show Live From Abbey Road, Abbey Road Studios, London, February 5 2011

MAIN IMAGE: Liam Gallagher performs as part of Beady Eye at Isle Of Wight Festival, June 12 2011

MAIN IMAGE: Liam Gallagher performs as part of Beady Eye at Leeds Festival - Day 2, West Yorkshire, England, August 27 2011

The album debuted at number three in the UK Albums Chart selling 66,817 in the first week. Eighteen months later, it had shifted 175,000 copies in total. With Oasis, Liam had sold out stadiums, arenas, festivals, now he was playing distinctly smaller venues – and the reviews weren't exactly favourable. *'Dull. . .with no grooviness. . . Beady Eye are going to have to raise their game if they want people to care about their future, and not just their singer's past,'* wrote one critic.

In March 2012, Liam stated that Beady Eye would start playing Oasis songs.

'The time is right now, without a doubt,' he said. *'We were always going to do it, but we thought the album needed to stand on its own. We've done some good gigs, we've done some s**t gigs. And it's time to drop them in now. Everyone else is. I feel they're just as much my songs as they are Noel's. And if people don't like it, go to the bar or f**k off. If they do like it, jump up and down, let's have a good time.'*

In August 2012, Beady Eye performed Wonderwall at the closing ceremony of the London 2012 Olympics. The band's second studio album, BE, was released on 12 June 2013. Once again, the reviews were mixed.

'This is a band that needs to sound a little blurry and blown-out,' read one. *'Beady Eye's broad strokes and bombastic flourishes are more satisfying when you can't make out the specifics. The pristine production only highlights how half-baked many of these songs are, especially lyrically.'*

The band embarked on a corresponding tour playing a 'secret gig' at Glastonbury. In contrast to his headlining spot with Oasis, Beady Eye featured as one of the first bands to open the festival. Liam stated it was a *'refreshing'* change. But he was talking it up. In reality, he missed playing the big venues. In 2014 Beady Eye disbanded. Liam tweeted that the band were *'no longer'* and thanked fans for their support. *'We weren't selling any tickets, and I thought, "I ain't f**king doing a third record to be fucking playing the 100 Club, I'd rather do f**king nothing','* he later said. *'It's either big or it's f**king nothing. I'm all or nothing.'*

His personal life was chaotic, too. In 2013, his five-year marriage to Nicole Appleton broke down when it came to light he had secretly fathered a daughter with New York journalist Liza Ghorbani in 2012. Liam was at his lowest ebb.

ABOVE: Beady Eye performing Wonderwall at the closing ceremony of the London 2012 Olympics

"She's a bit like my mam – because she doesn't take my s**t"

*'It was four f**king years of hell, with divorce lawyers and fucking all that bollocks,'* he said in 2017. *'And there was no gig. I felt like a shadow. … I was lost. I'd think, "F**k, how am I going to get out of this one?"'*

He credited new girlfriend, his former PA, Debbie Gwyther, with leading him back into the light – and the recording studio. It was Debbie's encouragement which persuaded him to become a solo artist.

*'She told me to f**king snap out of all the boozing and miserableness and all that, stop looking at the past and get in the f**king studio. She was a breath of fresh air, man. She sorted me right out. Me and her like to do the same things, like having a drink. We like having a laugh. I've met my match, I've met my soulmate. She's a bit like my mam – because she doesn't take my s**t.'*

Liam's first solo album, As You Were, was released to critical acclaim in October 2017. One review reading, *'As You Were is the legendary rocker at his very best.'*

*'I'm not here to change f**king rock'n'roll - I'm here to give people what they want and if that's boring, so be it,'* he said as he promoted the release. *'There's so much change in the world, and especially in the music business, I think it's nice to know you can rely on me. I like certain things to stay the f**king same. I think the music industry is better with me in it. That's not me being a bighead, it's just better.'*

Once again, Liam is playing sell out tours and stadiums – and neither the fans nor the critics can get enough of him.

'*Liam Gallagher positively owns the arena,*' narrated one review. '*You can't take your eyes off "our kid" or his close-ups on the monochrome screens which flank each side of the stage. Forget all that nonsense about his brother being the only one with the talent. This Gallagher has it in spades*'.

He seems happy with Debbie and has a good relationship with '*my lads*' – Lennon and Gene, now young adults. In spring 2017, he finally met elder daughter Molly Moorish for the first time and was reportedly in tears. However, Noel continues to loom large in his life as can be gleaned from his regular tweets. *#Mr Potato* is a favourite way of referring to his estranged brother. He also still seems bitter about the split.

'*He did me out, threw me under the fucking bus, and I won't forget that,*' says Liam. '*He split the band up and it meant the world to me. Just to further his career. So, me having a little pop at him when he f**king needs it, I don't give a f**k if his missus gets a bit of s**t on Twitter, or his f**king kid – welcome to my f**king world. I was getting s**t when you threw me under the bus and split the band up.*'

Yet it looks as if he'd be willing to reform Britpop's ultimate band in a heartbeat.

'*I would prefer to be speaking about an Oasis album than the Liam solo album,*' he says. '*And I know Noel Gallagher would. Because we're better together. I'm well aware of that, and so is he. But the bravado has slipped on occasion. I hope we make up. Not just for Oasis but for brothers – and our mam. Enough is enough now, I know I wind him up. I have put it out there enough times but I think he doesn't want to know.*

"I would prefer to be speaking about an Oasis album than the Liam solo album"

ABOVE: Liam Gallagher and John Squire perform at Fabrique, Milan, Italy, April 06 2024

'I hadn't had enough of Oasis, I'd had
enough of Liam...'

Noel Gallagher

Post Oasis, Noel launched a solo career under the banner Noel Gallagher's High Flying Birds. An album of the same name topped the charts in 2011. Concerts were upgraded from theatres to arenas. It wasn't Britpop glory, but Gallagher comfortably negotiated the post-Oasis wreckage.

But after the tour finished and he returned home to London in 2013, he found himself stuck.

'A dogsh**t year', he later described it. 'It was awful. I had glandular fever, then I went for my annual health check-up. And honest to God I felt all right when I went in, and the doctor made me feel like I was about to drop dead in the street when I came out. I got tinnitus in my ear, and I pulled two muscles in the back of my hand. Not from playing guitar - I cracked it on the side of something, and I bashed round the casing of the nerves. It was horrible. I couldn't even put my hand in my pocket. Then I went on holiday with the kids (by now he had two sons with second wife Sara). And I was getting out of a swimming pool with one of them in my hand and did my back in. Then my doctor put me on these tablets and told me that if I didn't take them I would virtually drop dead. I was taking them for months and they made me feel awful. So, I quit taking them and I felt great again. But I was thinking, the health game's a racket. So that was a terrible year. But then again, as soon as I got back to work, that took my mind off it, and I was all right.'

In the years since, Noel has continued to successfully write, play and tour with his High Flying Birds. The line-up presently includes former Oasis' bandmates – and Beady Eye alumni - Gem Archer and Chris Sharrock. He combines his career with a happy family life.

'When I'm in between tours and have f*** all to do, I sit around and I do become like a dad,' he's said. 'I don't really do a great deal. Music is my hobby. It's what I do. So, Sara is constantly on my case. She'll burst in from the gym, jogging on the spot. "What you doing today? You're watching Storage Hunters?" Me and my lads love that show!' And I'm thinking, "Ha, yes, I am – I've just been round the world for the last 18 months, so I am gonna watch Storage Hunters all day!" But she kind of badgers me into doing s**t. I go to the gym every day – I'm lucky enough to have a gym in my house.'

ABOVE: Noel Gallagher in Stockholm to promote his solo album "Noel Gallagher's High Flying Birds"

ABOVE: Noel Gallagher in Stockholm to promote his solo album "Noel Gallagher's High Flying Birds"

ABOVE: High Flying Birds perform on stage at Mad Cool Festival, Madrid, Spain, July 11 2019

ABOVE: High Flying Birds perfom on stage at Mad Cool Festival, Madrid, Spain, July 11 2019

Although his estranged brother has made noises about wanting to reform, Noel clearly has no intention.

'I get asked all the time every day when we'll get back together but Oasis is not going to get back together, I can predict with a 1000 per cent certainty that it is not going to happen. But I am not afraid of the legacy because it is secured with the first two Oasis albums. Listen, I read in the papers that Oasis has got unfinished business And I'm thinking, Well – whoever thinks that, I really f***ing pity them', because I left it all in the studio, I left it all on the stage. I had nothing more to give. That was it. And if there is unfinished business, I have finished all my business there. I have no more business with him. I play the songs because it is what people want to hear when I play live. And, why wouldn't I? I f***ing wrote all of them!'

He feels Oasis did all they could creatively.

'Any reunion would be great for my bank account, but it would be a year of my life—at least—where everything else would be on hold. And it would be miserable. Have you seen my brother's Twitter account? His life is just constant chaos, and now that's out there for all the world to see. Well, that's what it was like being in a band with him, 24/7. Why would I ever want to go back to that? If Oasis were ever to come back we couldn't be any bigger than we'd already been. There's no kudos in us selling out three nights at Wembley because we've already f**king done seven. The Stone Roses never played gigs of that magnitude. They came back and they were bigger than they'd ever been. So, it was justified. I'm never going to sell out Wembley Stadium on my own. Oasis could do 15 nights at the drop of a f**king hat but that's not what drives me now. I'm driven to make what I do now the best that it can be.'

ABOVE: Noel Gallagher's High Flying Birds perform on stage, May 1 2019, Rome, Italy

DISCOGRAPHY

ALBUMS

Highest Chart Position

	UK	US
Definitely Maybe (1994 Creation Records)	1	58
What's the Story Morning Glory (1995 Creation Records)	1	4
Be Here Now (1997 Creation Records)	1	2
Standing on the Shoulder of Giants (2000 Big Brother Records)	1	24
Heathen Chemistry (2002 Big Brother Records)	1	23
Don't Believe the Truth (2005 Big Brother Records)	1	12
Dig Out Your Soul (2008 Big Brother Records)	1	5

SINGLES

1994

	UK	US
Supersonic	31	11
Shakermaker	11	–
Live Forever	10	2
Cigarettes and Alcohol	7	–
Whatever	3	–

1995

	UK	US
Some Might Say	1	28
Roll With It	2	24
Wonderwall	2	1
Morning Glory	–	–

1996

	UK	US
Don't Look Back in Anger	1	10
champagne supernova	–	–

1997

	UK	US
D'You Know What I Mean?	1	4
Stand by Me	2	5

	UK	US
1998		
All Around the World	1	15
Don't Go Away	-	-
2000		
Go Let It Out	1	14
Who Feels Love?	4	-
Sunday Morning Call	4	-
2002		
The Hindu Times	1	-
Stop Crying Your Heart Out	2	-
Little By Little/She is Love	2	-
2003		
Songbird	3	-
2005		
Lyla	1	19
The Importance of Being Idle	1	-
Let There Be Love	2	-
2007		
Lord Don't Slow Me Down	10	-
2008		
The Shock of the Lightning	3	12
I'm Outta Time	12	-
2009		
Falling Down	10	-